The Stones of
TIR NAN OG

Neil C MacArthur

Kings House Publishing

The Stones of
TIR NAN OG

ISBN 0-9544849-1-6

Designed by twelveotwo
Cover photograph courtesy of Paul Norris

Published by
Kings House Publishing
Kings House Hotel, Balquhidder,
Perthshire FK19 8NY
SCOTLAND

Printed and bound in China by 1010 Printing International

DEDICATION

This book is dedicated to my wife Fiona and my daughter Mairi
who were absolutely no help whatsoever,
but they did put up with my ravings.

Also Black "Dan" and Eoin Neil Campbell from whom I have stolen.
But, I shall return.

And to all other Highland men, who when they realised
they were adult, rejected the whole philosophy
and remained as they were, children.

PRONUNCIATION GUIDE

There are a few Gaelic words used in this book
with which you may be unfamiliar and you are perfectly
entitled to pronounce them in any manner you wish,
but if you can remember as you read that "Bh" and "Mh"
in Gaelic are pronounced like "V" in English,
this I hope will add to your enjoyment of the book.

Neil C. MacArthur
Balquhidder, 2007

BHEITHIR'S CURSE

Bheithir weeps, and walks the lonely shore

That glows the deepest red.

Beside the waters she held so dear,

Beneath that bridge of grey,

The lamb is close, beside the cat,

Near the equine hill of dread.

Cursed by the Gods to wander now,

For she will ne'er be dead.

Anon.

FOREWORD

To those of you familiar with the unlikely comradeship
of Luath the deerhound and Tuppence the tree sparrow
in Neil C. MacArthur's first book, *The Hound's Tale*, this sequel
will come as a surprise and a delight. If, however, you are
unfamiliar with *The Hound's Tale*, may I suggest that it is as
essential to your enjoyment of *The Stones of Tir-nan-Og*
as *The Hobbit* is to *The Lord of the Rings*:
it is the seedbed of everything.

In this, the second part of Neil C. MacArthur's trilogy,
he works on a much broader canvas, an ambitious and vivid
display of story-telling in which his characters change landscapes
and even time itself. They face challenges and adventures
undreamed of when they first set out together in *The Hound's Tale*
to find the slow red squirrels of Balquhidder. Here they are
plunged deep into an ancient Celtic warrior-world that perhaps
still lies closer to the surface of twenty-first-century Scotland
than you are willing to believe.

Follow Luath and Tuppence in their quest for
The Stones of Tir-nan-Og; and believe.

Jim Crumley
Balquhidder, 2007

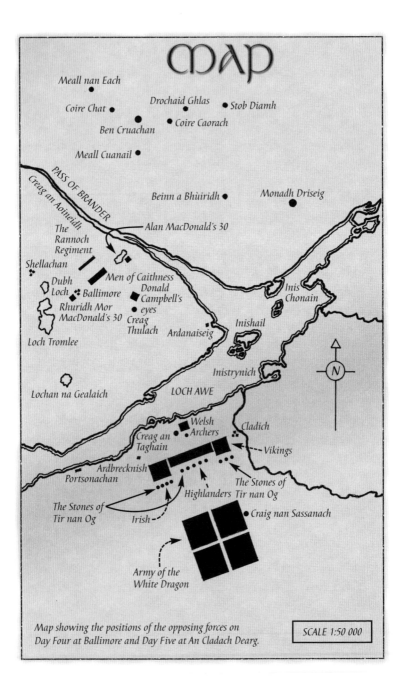

MAP

Meall nan Each

Coire Chat

Drochaid Ghlas

Stob Diamh

Ben Cruachan

Coire Caorach

Meall Cuanail

PASS OF BRANDER

Creag an Aoineidh

Beinn a Bhùiridh

Monadh Driseig

Alan MacDonald's 30

The Rannoch Regiment

Shellachan

Dubh Loch

Ballimore

Men of Caithness

Donald Campbell's eyes

Inis Chonain

Rhuridh Mor MacDonald's 30

Creag Thulach

Ardanaiseig

Inishail

Loch Tromlee

Lochan na Gealaich

Inistrynich

LOCH AWE

Welsh Archers

Cladich

Creag an Taghain

Vikings

Ardbrecknish

Portsonachan

The Stones of Tir nan Og

Highlanders

The Stones of Tir nan Og

Irish

Craig nan Sassanach

Army of the White Dragon

Map showing the positions of the opposing forces on Day Four at Ballimore and Day Five at An Cladach Dearg.

SCALE 1:50 000

CONTENTS

PREPARING

I returned the next morning to find Tuppence getting stuck into my breakfast.

"Hello Luath, I hope you don't mind but I started without you."

"I can see that you little squirt. Next time I want first go, alright? Got that?"

"Alright. But I didn't want it to go to waste."

"I suppose I'll come back one morning and find your cousin and all his cousins and all their cousins and aunties and uncles and mothers and fathers and grannies and grandpas. All preventing my breakfast from going to waste. Eh, Tuppence?"

"You're in a good mood this morning. This reminds me of the first time we spoke. You were away for a long time last night."

"Yes, Tuppence, about a year."

"Don't be daft, you went away last night and came home this morning. That's not a year, even I know that."

"I told you once before. A night in that hill can take a year."

"You weren't in Ben Shiann were you?"

"Yes."

"With the old hag?"

"Yes."

"The one that roasts sparrows over the fire?"

"I told you that was just a joke, and oh, she said you have to come the next time."

"Not on your life, never. It's too scary. Going away for a night and taking a year. I can't get my head round that one."

"You have a problem getting your head round the right way never mind actually utilising the old grey matter."

"What's grey matter?"

"Well, normal animals like human beings and me have located in our skulls an organ, which is squashy and grey in colour, and is called a brain. This is what we use to think with. If you have a good one you are called intelligent, if you have one like yours you are called Tuppence."

"You are in a bad mood this morning. I think I'll just go away. I don't know if I like you sometimes."

"Sometimes I don't know if I like me either, little friend. I'm sorry. I have other things on my mind."

"What things?"

"I can see trouble ahead Tuppence"

"Where?"

"In the hill, in Ben Shiann."

"Tell me Luath, tell me."

"I can't, you'll have to come with me the next time, I can't tell you out here."

"I'd be too scared to go in there."

"No you won't. You are a brave little fellow. Remember the kestrel?"

"Yes Luath. Alright then, the next time I'll come with you."

"But, don't tell your cousin."

"No, I won't."

"Oh, by the way, the old hag said she actually liked sparrows."

"That's nice, I feel better now, much better."

"Yes Tuppence, she said she liked sparrows so much, but the feathers keep getting caught between her teeth."

"Luath, I hate you! I really hate you!"

"That's just fine. You're going to need all the hate you've got inside that hill."

"I don't like the sound of that, I'm getting scared again."

"Tuppence, could you leave now? I have to rest. In two or three days I must go back."

"Where?"

"We are going on a mission."

"What's a mission?"

"It's one of these things the Salvation Army have. Why don't you push off now?"

"What's the Salvation Army?"

"Go away, get away from here, I'll see you tomorrow, get lost, tout-suite."

"Alright, see you tomorrow."

"Morning Luath, what a terrible day."

"Yes isn't it awful. I'm getting a bit damp in here; it hasn't stopped raining all night. I hope this isn't one of these summer showers that lasts from May till September."

"I hope not, it makes flying a bit tricky. High speed, high altitude flying is out today, I'm going for the low level stuff, under the trees. When you get hit on the wings with these big lumps of water it can spin you right round."

"That shouldn't make a lot of difference to you, should it? You never know where you're going anyway."

"You've got a point there Luath, but I always remember where I've been, I think."

"Right, you have obviously enjoyed my breakfast again. Now listen, in two days time we are leaving."

"Where are we going?"

"Into the hill, I told you yesterday."

"Yes, I know, but I thought you were joking."

"How often do you hear me joke?"

"Never Luath, never."

"Tuppence, I need your help. I told you we had a mission."

"I know, I am just trying to avoid the inevitable. I realise that you are serious, but I'm scared of getting hurt, or being plucked, or getting killed."

"You will not get hurt, or be plucked, or get killed as long as I am with you."

"Well that fills me with confidence, after the last time. Remember the last time we went to the Braes of Balquhidder, when you put my life in serious danger with the big hairy bull and the goat."

"Tuppence, it was my life in danger there, you were up in the air, flying about like an idiot, safe as houses."

"Alright, I give up. Do I have to go into the hill with you?"

"No, you have a choice. If you don't come with me, I'll pluck you myself. I'm asking for your help, Tuppence. I need a friend in there. It is a different world. I need someone I can rely on, someone that has the heart of Bruce."

"The heart of Bruce. What does that mean?"

"Tuppence, at one time this country was being invaded by foreigners and we needed a man of steel to drive these people out. The Bruce was there. He succeeded. I need him now and I have found him in you."

"I can't say no. Do you really think I can help you?"

"Tuppence, we all get one shot at this life. Are you going to listen to your cousin or are you coming with me into that hill?"

"I'm really scared now, I don't like this. I like flying about, eating midges and worms and your breakfast. I like it like this."

"What you like and what I like is not very important. Certain animals and certain people are chosen, and we have been chosen for this mission. I want you to go away now and I want you back here at midnight on the 13th of May and I want you to do some exercise. Press-ups and the like, I want you fit. You will need to be fit."

The wee bird left with a heavy heart and I felt sorry, but I needed him with me.

ᏟᏴᎬ ᏚᏟᎪᏒᏟ

The thirteenth arrived too quickly for Tuppence but he did come at midnight.

"Hello Luath."

"Hello little friend, how do you feel tonight?"

"Terrible."

"Yes, I understand, lets go."

We left An Carraig and headed across the main road, and across the bridge, and took a left at the fork. A hundred yards later we turned right, heading for the summit. I had to go the ground route. We followed the normal path up to the forest road then turned right and then a hundred and fifty yards later turned sharp left. It was plain sailing after that. Straight up and across the front of the hill.

Half a mile later we took a right turn, which leads straight up the front of Ben Shiann. It was pretty steep but I knew the route well. When we reached the summit we rested for two or three minutes. Now was the time to tell the little bird where we were actually going.

"Tuppence, this your last chance to go home."

"But I thought we were going into the hill, to see the old hag."

"When and if we go into the hill we will see the old hag. But when we enter this hill we are entering the Otherworld."

"What do you mean, the Otherworld?"

"Just what I say. We are not just going inside Ben Shiann. This is the entrance to the Otherworld."

"What's it like?"

"You will see shortly, but do you really want to come with me, my little friend? I need your help in there, but I'm not going to force you to come."

"I think I'll just go home then."

"Tuppence!"

"Alright, alright I'll come with you, as long as you promise I won't get hurt, or plucked, or killed."

"I promise. You're a volunteer now. Lets go."

We reached the summit without a problem. Ben Shiann is an extinct volcano with a plug of igneous rock protruding out of the top. We went over the summit and started to descend the west side to a little corrie covered in rough grass and heather. At the back of the corrie is a big round rock. I showed Tuppence how to roll this rock to the right, to gain access to the hill.

We stepped inside then shut off the entrance.

"I'm scared Luath."

"So am I Tuppence. It always gives me the creeps when I come in here."

It was dark for a few seconds then our eyes adjusted. Then we started seeing lights.

"Where do we go now?"

"Just a minute. Just wait."

All of a sudden there was light everywhere.

"We are on our way now. Down."

We descended quickly in a great spiral. Down and down we went, we had gone about as far down as we had climbed on the outside.

"Luath, Luath! I hear something. I think I'm going to panic."

"Don't be daft, it's nothing."

"But I can hear a voice, a woman's voice."

"Yes my little friend, it's a woman's voice. I know her well, I will introduce you."

All of a sudden she appeared.

"Tuppence, this is Ishbel. The old hag."

"Hello Tuppence. I've heard so much about you, I feel I almost know you already."

"Luath, You told me about an old hag that roasts sparrows over open fires…"

"This is she."

"Hello, Ishbel… d-d-d-do you eat sparrows?"

"What do you think Tuppence?"

"What do I think? I think this dog-hound thing has told me a pack of lies. You are the most beautiful woman I've ever seen in my life."

"Tuppence, don't listen to everything Luath tells you."

"But he is my hero."

"Luath is a hero to a lot of people and animals, but heroes, Tuppence, heroes are not always as they seem."

"I don't understand."

"My little bird, in this world there are heroes and villains and sometimes it is very difficult to tell them apart."

"You mean Luath is a villain."

"No. Tuppence. I mean Luath will do things that sometimes do not seem heroic."

"I'm totally confused. I was happy in the other place, eating midges, flying about and having fun. Now I'm in a place I can't understand."

"You will not understand till you return home."

"When will that be?"

"It will not be as long as you think."

"Have I arrived in hell?"

"No. Hell has no dangers like this place."

"We'll that's really cheered me up. Thank you!"

"Tuppence listen. Luath has brought you here for a reason. He has chosen you because no other animal or human can do what you can do."

"Oh yes. All I do is fly about eating midges and speak to my cousin in Balquhidder, and Luath has virtually told me that he's an imbecile."

"Don't judge him too harshly, little bird. From what he has told me about you, I think you are the only other creature in the world that he admires."

"He admires me? You're joking! That big hairy dog only thinks of himself."

"He's a hound isn't he?"

"Yes, Ishbel, he's a hound. Do I have to follow him?"

"No, I will take you home right now if you want. But if you leave now, this world might tear itself apart and all of us with it."

"And if I stay, what then?"

"If you stay, we have a chance, a slim chance, but a chance."

"Just a chance?"

"Yes, just a chance."

"So what do I do now?"

"You will go with that big hairy hound and deliver this world from the grip of terror."

"I don't know if I can do this."

"He will look after you, and you will look after him. You are brothers."

"Thank you very much. I have a big brother that's a hairy dog-hound thing, that can't fly, and I'm a sparrow."

"A perfect combination. Couldn't be better."

I decided it was time I interrupted this little tête-à-tête.

"You two have been talking a long time. We'll have to get going."

"Ishbel, what's the news?"

"You have to report to the Ard Righ as soon as possible."

"Where is he?"

"The army or what's left of it is retreating up Glen Ogle. They passed here last night and Aedan Bhan came here himself to talk."

"What did he say?"

"He told me he needed his messenger now. You are the messenger. You are late."

"I know Ishbel. We will make the time up. I now have my messenger with wings."

This time the messenger with wings interrupted.

"I heard that! Army retreating...you didn't tell me, you were taking me to war."

"If I had told you that, you wouldn't have come."

"No! Never!"

"Well you're here now, so it doesn't matter."

"Oh, so it doesn't matter, you big dope. You take me from a happy life in peace and you bring me to another world where there is war."

"I cannot face this alone. I need you here, I need wings."

"So I am your wings?"

"Yes, you are my wings."

"So I am the messenger's wings."

"Tuppence, you are the messenger's wings."

"I will not forget. And if I get hurt or plucked or killed I will never forgive you, never!"

"If one feather on your scrawny, little body is damaged, or you are plucked or you are killed, I will share your fate."

"Oh that's alright then, let's go."

The Otherworld

With a quick farewell to the most beautiful hag in the Otherworld, we emerged from the foot of Ben Shiann into the sunlight of another time. It was a beautiful morning in May and sun showered her reckless rays on the Perthshire hills.

"This place doesn't look any different from the place we left."

"It's not, it's still Ben Shiann, and you are still in Highland Perthshire. It is just in a different time."

"I can't say I understand."

"It does confuse me too, at times Tuppence. But look around, there are some differences. Can you spot them?"

"There don't seem to be any tarmac roads. Oh, and where are the Sitka spruce trees?"

"Yes Tuppence, there are no plantations here."

"Why's that?"

"It's because the Forestry Commission hasn't managed to find a way in yet. Thank goodness."

"I'll drink to that."

"Right Tuppence, you must be careful, keep your eyes open and listen. You must listen. You will see and hear things you won't believe.

We must hurry. If Aedan Bhan and the army passed here last night heading for Glen Ogle, they will be over the pass by now and descending into Glen Dochart."

"Do we follow them?"

"No. There is a short cut into Glen Dochart. Let's go."

After a little while Tuppence said:

"This is the same way we came to find the squirrels."

"You're right. We just head for the church as we did before."

"Do you think Hamish is still in the field? Remember when he went through the dyke?"

"I remember. But I don't think he'll be there."

"Why not Luath. Why not?"

"Hamish hasn't been born yet."

"Don't be daft, that's just silly. I saw him just the other day, frightening the living daylights out a bunch of fishermen from Falkirk."

"I told you, we're in another time, and another world"

"You're serious aren't you?"

"Yes, deadly serious."

"I don't think I like the sound of that. I thought that was a story just to frighten me."

"It's not a story, but I'll bet you're a bit scared now. Get up you stupid bird. Get up."

"Sorry Luath, fell out of the sky. I'll walk, I'll just walk. It's such a lovely day. I think I'll just walk."

"If you walk it's going to take days to get to Glen Dochart."

"I hope it takes f...f...f...flipping weeks."

"Come on, we haven't even seen anything yet, nothing's happened yet."

"But it will Luath, won't it?"

"Oh yes. It will!"

We pushed on to Balquhidder Kirk, familiar ground, memories of squirrels and goats and bulls and kestrels, and then Tuppence said:

"Where now?"

"From here we're in different territory. Keep left of the church and keep east of the burn, and up through Kirkton Glen."

"The church doesn't look the same, does it?"

"No. It's not the same. I don't even think it's a church just now. There are no Christians here at the moment."

"When do the Christians arrive?"

"I don't know, but they will get here too, no doubt."

"Do you not like Christians then?"

"I can take them or leave them my little friend, let's just say I have an ambivalent attitude towards them."

"You know some fantastic words don't you? I don't know what ambivalent means but I'm going to remember that one, and one day I'm going to use it."

"You do that. Sometimes its nice to hide behind a big word or half a dozen big words, or a dozen big words but other times its nice to have no words at all and no protection. Sometimes its nice just to be yourself."

"Do these Christians know anything about sparrows?"

"I'm not sure, but I've never seen a sparrow getting a Christian funeral."

"Neither have I."

"Luath."

"Yes Tuppence."

"What is a funeral?"

"A funeral is one of those things you get when you die."

"Die. What's die?"

"Di is a Welshman."

"Don't be daft. What's die?"

"Die, is when you stop breathing."

"We'll never stop breathing, will we?"

"No, we'll never stop breathing. We are immortal!"

"What's immoral?"

"No, not immoral, the word is immortal."

"I don't really care, immoral or immortal, I'm ready for this war now."

"Are you sure?"

"Yes, I'm sure."

"You're a brave little fellow. Either that or you're stupid."

"I'm not stupid! I'm intelligent, confident, assured, rational, suave, dominating and handsome."

"No, Tuppence. You're just a wee sparrow with a BIG heart." We went up the glen with the burn on our left through open woodland of oak and ash and birch and rowan. We were heading for Ledcharrie in Glen Dochart. At the highest point we passed Lochan an Eireannach then followed the Ledcharrie Burn down between the two peaks of Creag Loistge and Creag Ghlas.

We saw no one, not a soul, not a living creature. We could have been the only two left alive on this bleak earth. We did not speak. Tuppence kept his own counsel and I mine. Our journey was not long in miles but it felt eternal. This space in time helped me little, this space could sever our bond, this space was torture, the kind of twisted torture you reserve for yourself and those closest to you. Tuppence wore his fear like an aura and my resolve began to wane. What have I done? This little bird trusts me. This little bird has followed me across the Styx. I am repaying his faith with what? With almost certain catastrophe, with death and with my foolish unholy pride. I decided I would take him home and he would be safe.

The First Sighting

"Tuppence."

"Yes?"

"I think we should go home."

"Wait a minute, Luath, what's that?"

"What's what?"

"That sound."

"I don't hear anything."

"Listen. Listen, you told me to listen when we got in here."

"I hear it now. Yes, I hear it."

With a mile to go of the seven from Balquhidder we heard it.

We heard the sound that raises little hairs on the back of your neck and sends little shivers down your spine and makes you tremble a little and sets your blood on fire, coursing through your veins like a tempest from Tarvos Taranos and it prepares you at least a little for what's ahead. You have the tremblings of valour, battle is close and you cannot go home, not any more. The die is cast. The bridges are smouldering now and to leave would condemn you to a life of purgatory and regret.

There was no mistaking the sound, there was no mistaking the instrument, and there was no mistaking the tune. War or Peace.

"Tuppence, how do you feel? Tuppence."

"Yes, I feel it, I feel it strangely. I have never felt this before, but I'm not scared, its not fear, but it's awful like it."

"It is awful like it, isn't it? Fear has many companions, my little friend, but control is its master. We'll descend a little more and conceal ourselves and watch as they pass and I will explain a few things to you."

We found a spot just above Ledcharrie and looked to the east for the first signs of their approach.

"I thought you were to report to the High King immediately, Luath?"

"We will see Aedan Bhan when they camp for the night. That will be soon enough."

The sound of the great Highland war pipes grew stronger. Then the first sightings. Sun glinting on steel along the south bank of the Dochart. Then figures, banners, colour! Riotous, raucous, unnerving colour! The army had all the appearance of victors with the sweet smell of triumph in their nostrils. Yet they had just tasted defeat. What kind of men were these? What kind of men conduct themselves like this after a string of bloody rebuffs?

They grew closer and closer and closer. Who in their right mind would face these men, and who in any state of mind would fight them? Tuppence spoke:

"There are an awful lot of them. There must be millions."

"Not millions, but there are thousands. I just hope there are enough thousands."

"I didn't know there were that many men in the Highlands."

"These men are not just from the Highlands. They are from all over the western seaboard."

"But I thought this army was retreating?"

"It is."

"But they don't look like they're running away."

"They're not running away, they are retreating and regrouping in order to fight again. But this is not just one army. These are the remnants of four armies that have eventually joined forces because separately they were taking a pasting."

"Who were they all fighting?"

"They have been fighting a foe that does not retreat even under the fiercest onslaught, a foe that knows only one direction, (forward), a foe whose heart is as black as the standard they fight under, a foe whose only thought is conquest, a foe whose only pleasure is destruction, a foe whose only prayer is utter desolation."

"They sound like a cheery bunch. Where are they from then?"

"They are from far beyond the Southern Channel, from exactly where none of us knows, but we know where they are just now."

"What are they called?"

"We call them Darkness my little friend, The Fiends of Darkness, but they have many names in many places. The Norsemen call them the Army of Eternal Night and the Welsh call them The Men of the White Dragon and the Irish, the Irish just call them Blackhearts. But what ever we call them Tuppence, they are the most formidable enemy ever to set foot on these islands."

"And how many men have they got?"

"About forty thousand…give or take a couple of thousand."

"And how many have we got?"

"About thirteen thousand give or take a couple of hundred."

"Thirteen? Thirteen thousand? You've got to be kidding."

"No, I'm serious."

"That's not a fair fight, I'm going home. Bye now."

"Tuppence, come back here. Its not that bad, it's only odds of three to one."

"I know that, but they've got the three and we've got the one. I wouldn't fight three blue tits myself."

"But we might get some help."

"And where are we going to get help round here may I ask? Look round about. The place isn't exactly swarming with thirty thousand buckshee warriors just itching for a fight, is it now? Maybe there's ten thousand behind that hill and maybe there's ten thousand at the back of that hill and there could be another ten thousand to the rear of that one over there just hanging about on the off chance of war. Come on Luath, this is just ridiculous, just plain stupid."

"No, Tuppence we will get help somewhere else. That is our mission!"

"Oh yes and where are we going to get help?"

"I don't quite know how to tell you this."

"Come on. Spit it out, where are we – you and me – going to get Help with a capital H?"

"From the Gods!"

"What?! What?! Have you got a screw loose? Have you gone completely off your rocker? Should you not be locked up in a darkened room somewhere with a yellow plastic bag over your head, away from here, a long way from here? From the Gods! Oh yes, that'll be right."

"Well, that's the idea and its up to us to pull something off. Its up to us to create the circumstances for this army to be victorious."

"You sound like a salesman, Luath, you sound like some silly ass who is trying to flog me free access to the internet or some clown who's trying to give me something for nothing to clean my toilet."

"My mother warned me, she warned me when I was a little chick in the nest. She would say to me: 'Never go with strangers, always eat up all your midges and never go near weird dogs.' Well I'm in it now! Right up to my neck. Maybe I should write to her: 'Dear Mother, just a little note to let you know that I've joined the Army. Yes, mother, that's right the Army. But don't worry, we have thirteen thousand men and the enemy has only got three times more. Luath says it's alright. We are going to get help. Where are you going to get help I can hear you say? Luath says we can get help from the Gods, all these Celtic and Norse Gods that abound in these parts. It's just a piece of cake, like winning the lottery. Personally I don't have a problem with it. Who is Luath? I can hear you ask. Luath is my best friend, and he is a weird dog. I know you warned me about weird dogs when I was in the nest but everything will be all right. My friend Luath told me so. Love and Kisses, Tuppence.'"

"Come on, it isn't really that bad is it?"

"Of course it's that bad. It's worse than that bad. It's impossible. That army down there is going to get annihilated, and you and I with it."

"It is not impossible Tuppence. It's very close to it, but nothing is impossible. Let's discuss this later. The army is close now. Let's watch as they go past and I'll let you know who they are and where there are from."

"Alright, but after that I'm going home."

ÒONALÒ

In a great sweep the army came past us, the out-runners first, twenty or thirty men in an arrowhead formation, about two hundred yards in front of the main body.

"What are they doing, Luath?"

"They are just making sure there's no one ahead and there are no nasty surprises in store."

"What do you mean?"

"I mean they are ensuring a clear passage for this army. If the Blackhearts were in front they would need to know rapidly in order to take the necessary action. Now, you see them, you tell me about them."

"What do you mean?"

"You tell me what you see."

"I don't really know what you mean, but I'll tell you what I see. Men, thirty men moving, not slowly, not quickly, but with urgency with light measured paces, covering the ground easily, lightly clad, lightly armed, alert, wary, young, between fourteen and eighteen years, determined, wearing dark tartans and darker looks, the eyes of the army, and not one of them saw us on the way past, did they?"

"Ciamar a tha sibh an diugh, Luath agus Tuppence?"

"Who's that? Where is he? I can't see him. How did he get here? How does he know my name? Luath I'm scared."

"He's behind us. He's seventeen, wearing dark tartans and a darker look and he's a Campbell and he covers the ground easily and he's determined and he has a dirk and he's urgent and he has the speed of the deer and the eye of the hawk and he's a friend and his name is Donald, and Tuppence, don't be scared, we're on his side. It's good to see you, Donald."

"Luath, you're needed, you're needed now, you know that of course. Aedan Bhan has a troubled mind, he's struggling to hold this army together, we have a battle looming and he's looking for you and this little bird. He is on the verge...you know what I mean."

"I surely do and I will come to Aedan Bhan tonight when you set up camp."

"I've been watching out for you since Loch Lubnaigside, Luath. I knew you had to be close. Your presence has lifted my heart and you have your little winged warrior with you."

"Yes, this is he, this is Tuppence."

"It will be very interesting to have you in this army, Tuppence. Welcome to Hell."

"Thank...Thank you, Donald. Is this really Hell?"

"No my little comrade it just feels like it sometimes. No, not sometimes, all the time.

I'll have to get going, Luath. The left flank is short of a pair of eyes at the moment.

We'll be camped at Inverardran tonight, just below Creag na h-iolaire, Eagle Rock, at the head of Glen Falloch and I'll tell Aedan to expect two visitors. See you both then. Decisions will be made later."

Donald slipped away as quietly as he had appeared.

"He nearly frightened me out of my feathers, Luath. How did he manage to sneak up on us like that? And did you see the look in his eye? He's a scary man, he looks like he's seen things I haven't."

"He has seen things you haven't and he's done things people only talk about in whispers. When that young man is about, it's the others you should fear for."

"Why?"

"He's a handy boy with a blade, a blade of any length, and he is the best friend you and I will know in this world. They call him Donald an't Sgian, Donald the Knife.

"The main body is here now, Tuppence. See that little group, mounted on garrons? Aedan Bhan is at the front, in the centre, astride that awkward beast Fergus. He's the most stubborn animal I've ever met in my life. The ones on his flanks are the leaders of the other forces. We'll no doubt meet them all in the fullness of time. Behind them are the Druids with their six colours, and behind them are the standard bearers, four great standards one for each of the armies, keeping up a steady pace. They are the leadership, Tuppence, these are the people men die for, these are the people men hate and these are the people men love and these are the people that will decide what our fate will be. What do you think?"

"Are they good at their job?"

"If history is anything to go by, no."

"Then why are they leaders?"

"Most by an accident of birth, some by a quirk of fate, some by treachery, some by corruption, but all of them are here now and not somewhere else."

"I suspect Luath, you're not really taken with them then?"

"No. I'd put Donald an't Sgian, above them all."

"Then why is Donald not the Ard Righ then?"

"Donald is seventeen, has no wealth, no power, no position, no backing, no clout. He's still only a boy."

"But you would support him, wouldn't you?"

"I would, but this story is not finished yet. Let's watch the men that will shed blood."

Three great columns came into view on the flood plain of the Dochart. Side by side they swept past, Highlanders in the middle directly behind the leadership, five thousand at least, dark and red and fair, haughty, uncompromising, colourful, bristling with hate, bristling with pride, bristling with weapons – and uncomfortable, for on each flank marched men they would sooner fight against than fight with.

On their left flank were four thousand from the Emerald Isle – all the provinces in Ireland had men in this army – men from Leinster, men from Munster, men from Connacht and even MacDonalds from the glens of Antrim in Ulster. They shared blood and language and history, but they also shared battles and wives and sweethearts and likes and dislikes and enemies and colour and panache.

On the Highlanders' right were the Norsemen, tall, fair and as warlike as the others, but slightly less colourful than the Celts, leather jerkins, close fitting breeks with leather strappings, glorious helmets and weapons that a mason would use. Not for them Ferrara's blades, but hammers and axes and short swords. And their decoration seemed less stylish, not the flowing curves of Celtic creation. But they too had men from the Hebrides, MacLeods and Morrisons and men from Orkney and Shetland and Bogence and Hardanger and every fjord on the coast of Norway. They numbered about three thousand, but would rather be in long ships than marching.

But behind these three great columns came the men that made the whole army uneasy – one thousand from Cymru, singing incessantly, dark square men with longbows and sharp tongues and red dragons tattooed on their hearts, with allies from Cornwall and Brittany. And they have Basques with them from the Iberian Peninsula. How they got involved, who knows?

"Do you think they will all hold together till they meet the Blackhearts, Luath?"

"That is the task for the leadership, but I do know one thing, if there's not a battle with The Army of Eternal Night very soon, this uneasy alliance will end in bloodshed."

The main body of the Army had now passed in a great curve sweeping round the bend in the Dochart at Luib, heading for Inverardran and a night's rest. Close behind followed the supplies, nearly fifty garrons laden with sacks and barrels and tenting, weaponry and clothing, tended by young boys, who encouraged and pushed and harassed their charges forwards. Behind them came the rearguard, another thirty men of Argyll like young Donald, with eyes half turned to the rear, making very sure this Army had no unwanted followers.

"Is that their only food, Luath? It doesn't seem enough for so many men."

"That's some of it, the rest they will get en route. They will take deer from the forest and lift cattle from the pastures, as they go."

"I'm getting a bit peckish, Luath. What's in the sacks and barrels?"

"There will be oatmeal in the sacks, and the barrels, well that just depends on how lucky you are."

"What do you mean lucky?"

"Well my little friend, some barrels will have salt herring in them."

"Oh! Yuck, Luath, I can't eat that stuff. Fish in salt! How could any sane bird eat that? What about the other ones?"

"Some barrels will have salt beef in them."

"How disgusting. Nobody in this day and age eats salt beef. Is there nothing worth eating in this man's army?"

"Remember, Tuppence, you're not in this day and age, you're in someone else's day and age."

"What about the other barrels, there must be something I can eat, surely?"

"How about salted pork or we have, salted venison or I could give you salted mutton, but we also have snails for the Bretons."

"That's more like it. And what are they done in?"

"Salt!"

"Och Luath, you're just pulling my leg now."

"Okay. When I knew you were coming I had a word with our catering suppliers and I ordered midges for you, best quality, top of the range Kyle of Lochalsh gourmet midges."

"Oh! Luath, that's wonderful, I've never had Kyle of Lochalsh gourmet midges before, in fact I've never had gourmet midges before. Come to think of it, I don't know what gourmet means. What does it mean?"

"It means there the ones all the best chefs use."

"That's marvellous, Luath, and what are they done in?"

"A saline solution!"

"You're a complete b...b...b...swine, Luath. Sometimes I think that's all you're good at – taking the p...p...p...micky out of me. I'll just go and find my own food."

"There's a little sack on one of these garrons. It's the best I could do. It's bird seed and it's for you alone, Tuppence, and there's no salt near it, you can have some before we see Aedan Bhan tonight."

"Luath. Thank you, you big fool."

"That's alright, but Tuppence there are some casks with something else in them, there are some there with an amber liquid in them and it's called uisge beatha – the water of life."

"But what is it, Luath?"

"Whisky, Tuppence, whisky. Anyway, we'll just follow the Army a good way behind. We do not need to be involved at the moment. Our time will come. We'll just enjoy the walk or the flight and we will get there when all the work is done, and all the tents are up and the leaders are feeling important again, after actually having to get off their rear ends and do something. We will appear and eat, and then, we will permit them some of our time and if they require our help, we might give it or we might not."

"Luath, you're scaring me, I've never heard you speak like this before, it's almost as if you do not like them. What's wrong?"

"There is nothing wrong; this is the way I am. This is me. Do you think I have come here to be used by the collection of cretins who are the leadership of this army? With your help we will show this army how to be triumphant, but they will never know."

ÐREAÐING

6

"Let's find the garrons Tuppence, let's get you fed. I'm sure Donald will be there."

When we found the garrons a young boy came running past, I shouted:

"Laddie, give me a hand here."

"Oh, Luath! What can I do for you?"

"What's your name?"

"My name's Euan."

"Well Euan, there is a little sack in Army provisions with the word 'Tuppence' on it. Have you seen it?"

"I think I have."

"That little sack is for my friend Tuppence. Could you find it and bring it to us as soon as you possibly can?"

"Right Luath, I'll do that."

Within the blink of an eye he was back carrying the little sack. Tuppence was hungry. Donald found us. It was the best place for us to talk, amongst the garrons and the grooms.

"Have you had enough to eat yet, Tuppence? I need your ears too."

"Donald, give me an assessment of our chances in this battle, against The Blackhearts. You've fought them before."

"Do you want honesty, Luath?"

"Yes of course I do."

"Slim."

"You're being slightly over optimistic are you not? We have no chance. What do we do? How do we turn this round? What would you do Donald? And what would you do Tuppence?"

Donald took his time to answer but Tuppence was quicker.

"How the devil would I know?"

Donald said:

"Well, we have potent weapons in this Army. We have one thousand Welsh bowmen who can shower death on any Army from three hundred yards away."

"What else?"

"Well, we have Norse Berserkers, who are just the most fearsome and intimidating foe you will ever face."

"What else?"

"We have our own men – Highlanders, the Highland charge, few armies face that one twice."

"What else, Donald?"

"We have the Irish."

"And what have they got?"

"Just complete mayhem, Luath. They totally confuse the enemy into thinking they are defeated."

"And Tuppence, what do you think is our most potent weapon?"

"It's got to be the Kyle of Lochalsh gourmet midges."

"Don't be such a dope. Donald, when you dream at night what do you dream of?"

"I dream of battles and wars."

"And what else?"

"I dream of women too."

"And when you dream of battles, what are you like in these battles?"

"I am the greatest warrior there has ever been, I am like Sentanta, the Hound of Coulann."

"And are you ever defeated?"

"No, never."

"And are you ever wounded?"

"Yes, often, but they are always superficial, just flesh wounds."

"And do these wounds ever prevent you from defeating your foe?"

"No. Why do you ask, Luath?"

"And when you dream of women, what do they look like?"

"Just beautiful and gifted and shining."

"And what do you look like?"

"I'm handsome, brave and irresistible, but why do you ask these questions?"

"Tell me now then, Donald, what is our most potent weapon? And, you tell me Tuppence, what is our most potent weapon?"

"Luath, I do not know what you're driving at. We have an army of heroes out there and I would die with them all. But we lack numbers that is our trouble, numbers, we do not have enough men, and I do not understand what you mean."

"And I haven't the foggiest idea what you're talking about, and Luath, I think you've just flipped, and I think I'll just go home and talk to my cousin. At least he talks sense."

"Tuppence, you just listen! Donald, you have just answered the question I have asked. The most potent weapon this army has is imagination."

"I don't know if I understand."

"Donald, when you dream you win; the battle, the war, the woman. This army, has to dream of winning, it's got to use its imagination. We do not need more men, all we need are our stories, our heroes. Our past is our future, we can win this battle if we believe we can."

"I know what you're saying, Luath, but how can we make this happen?"

"I still haven't got the foggiest what you're both on about," said Tuppence, "but Donald, you're beginning to believe him aren't you?"

"Under the circumstances, Tuppence, I don't really think we have a lot of options."

"So you're both with me then?"

"Yes, I'm with you till the bitter end."

"And, Tuppence what about you?"

"It doesn't make any sense to me at all, I can't see how an army can win a battle by dreaming, but who am I to argue? I'm with you I suppose."

"Right, let's make it all happen. Donald, I need a word with the chief Druid before I speak to Aedan Bhan, can you take me to him?"

"Surely. Follow me. I'll show you his tent."

"What about me?"

"You wait with the grooms and eat your seed, we'll be back, shortly."

⊂ḥe ⱭRȺ RIGḥ

We were back with Tuppence inside an hour.

"What did you want to see the chief Druid for?"

"I wanted to tell him what to do."

"But isn't the chief Druid the most powerful man in the country after the High King?"

"Yes what of it?"

"You told the second most powerful man in the country what to do?"

"Yes."

"And how did he take it?"

"After I mentioned Christianity, he was most co-operative."

"That's a bit sneaky, Luath, isn't it, but I like it, I really like it. What's his job then?"

"Oh, just to increase the Gods' profile, hold little ceremonies within the camp, tell the men that the Gods have promised help and that our envoys are presently meeting with the Gods to discuss the nature of the assistance to us in this forthcoming battle. So as you can see all the little Druids running about the place have got to work very quickly."

"Who are these envoys then, Luath?"

"That's you and me, dope. Now, Donald, you and your lads being the eyes and ears of this army must know men in all sections of this alliance?"

"Certainly, Luath, I myself am particularly friendly, with a bunch of Berserkers from Bergen."

"You do seem to keep some strange company sometimes. Still, never mind. Can you and your boys seek out all the seanachies and storytellers and encourage them to tell their tales to every one in this outfit that will listen, no matter what part of the army they are from, starting now?"

"I'll get going straight away. How much encouragement do you want us to give them?"

"Could you maybe go canny, Donald? Leave your dirks behind and we'll see you in the morning, before we leave. We'll go and see Aedan Bhan now."

"Tuppence let's go and meet a King. Have you ever met a King before?"

"No, I don't think so, not that I'm aware of."

"Is there not a King of the Sparrows?"

"I don't know. Maybe there is..."

"Well, my little friend, if there is not a King of the Sparrows already, I suggest that you apply for the job?"

"But, where would I apply, who would I contact, and how does that all work?"

"I think the easiest way is to declare yourself King and then just field the questions, declare war on the opposition and hang any sparrow that gets in the way. That seems to work well for humans and it will amaze you how many followers you will accumulate very quickly. What do you think?"

"Yes, I'm all for that; you're are now talking to The King of the Sparrows. But wait a minute, is not Aedan Bhan, Ard Righ, the High King?"

"Yes, he is. And that's a fact."

"Well in that case I, Tuppence Montanus the First do declare myself The High King of the Sparrows and other little birdies, like blue tits and wrens and the finches and the buntings and the warblers and the...."

"Steady, Tuppence, let's take one step at a time, High King of the Sparrows, sounds pretty good at the moment, doesn't it?"

"Yes, it does, but in time, in time, I will become King of all the wee birds, and look after them and tend to their needs, and I might even set up a health service for them and an insurance scheme and a pay as you earn facility and ..."

"Save it, Tuppence, just save it for later. What I need at the moment is a King with me as I meet a King. Do you understand or not?"

"Yes, I understand. I just got carried away a little bit. All this power makes you slightly mad, doesn't it? I mean, I've never had so much power before, I just got carried away. There's no harm in it, is there?"

"With you, Tuppence, there's no harm, because there's no harm in you. But what would that do to the average clown on this earth, be it bird, be it hound or be it human? It's a good thing that most of them have never tasted the power you have just now."

"Yes, thank the Gods for that."

"Anyway, my little friend, you're a King now so I expect you to behave like a King."

"What is that you're saying minion?"

"Talk that way again to me and I'll snap your neck, understand?"

"I'm just practicing, just trying to get the hang of it, how to talk down to all earthly creatures."

"We'll discuss this later, just get your a...a...a...self into gear, would you, this meeting is vital. Understand?"

"Right, Luath, I've got it, I'm a King, I'm a King, I will act like a King."

We approached the guards outside Aedan Bhan's tent.

"HALT! State your names and your business."

"I am the Hound of Aedan's Messages and I have with me the High King of the Sparrows. Our presence was requested."

"Och it's Luath and Tuppence, Angus, let them past and I'll tell Aedan they're here at last!"

Aedan Bhan had his back to us, arms folded, deep in thought, silent. He wasn't the tallest of men, but he was squarely built, fair hair to the shoulder, powerful, strong forearms and hands like a farmer. He was in his mid-thirties, had a quick temper and a voice like Thor's thunder, his face was honest and strong and his eyes a piercing blue. He wore a thin circlet of gold round his forehead, the only indication of his rank. Until he spoke that is.

I whispered to Tuppence.

"Brace yourself!"

I had just got the words out when Aedan swung round and in one movement buried his fist into the little table between us. The table did not have the strength to withstand the impact and shattered like a glass. Pieces of timber scattered like confetti.

"Where the hell have you been, what have you been up to, what took you so long and where the hell is the King and the army you promised, eh Luath? Where are they?"

"Well, Aedan I have the King with me and the army is waiting to be summoned."

"Where is the King?"

"This is he."

"That's a bloody sparrow, that is not a King, that is a sparrow. Look, a short brown, feathered thing with a beak, wings and skinny legs. That, Luath, that, is a sparrow!"

"But he's the King of the Sparrows."

"And how is the King of the Bloody Sparrows going to help us? Maybe we can peck the Army of Darkness to death or into surrender, is that it? What a cunning strategy. I would never have thought of that, not in a million years."

Then Tuppence spoke up.

"May I be permitted to speak in this company, Aedan Bhan?"

"Speak then!"

"I come here as High King of the Sparrows and I expect to be given the courtesy that I give to you as the High King of the Albannach. I expect to be listened to and if you do not like what you hear I will leave and return home."

"I have a war to fight and an army to control and a country to save and a world to preserve. What do you know of these matters?"

"It matters little what I know of these matters but it matters greatly that I know these matters exist."

"I do you a disservice, little bird. What is your name?"

"Tuppence."

"Tuppence? What a bloody stup…. good name, yes, that's a good name. Well, Tuppence, if you can help, I can listen. Tell me what you can do."

"How many fighting men do you lead, Aedan?"

"About thirteen thousand."

"And the enemy?"

"About forty thousand."

"If every one of your thirteen thousand fought like three men, would you go into battle with confidence?"

"If every one fought like three I would take on the world, tonight."

"Do you believe in the Gods?"

"Well… well…yes, yes I do."

"But do the Gods believe in you, Aedan Bhan, High King of the Albannach?"

"Most definitely, without doubt, the Gods believe in me."

"In that case I will ally my Kingship with yours and bring my forces to bear upon your enemy."

"I admire your words, Tuppence, I admire your bravery, and I admire your commitment, you are indeed a King. Our armies will join forces and our enemy will know nothing of it, till it is beyond their control, on the field of battle.

Leave now my friends, be back early tomorrow, for I have the eyes of the Army out tonight."

We left Aedan's tent to look for a place to rest till the morning.

"Tuppence, I asked you to behave like a King in there, in that tent with Aedan Bhan. You acquitted yourself with the dignity of a thousand Kings, I was proud."

"Luath, I believe now, I believe we can defeat this army, I have committed myself to Aedan Bhan. We must find a way, we must speak to the Gods, and we must make this army three times stronger, if it's the last thing we do."

"It's been a hard road, Tuppence, has it not? We must shake off the dust of that dull world we left behind. We have a mission and an almighty battle ahead. You and I are ready for war."

"Luath. We are brothers, are we not?"

"Tuppence, we have to let our imaginations fly tomorrow, and we will change the course of history."

ᴛʜᴇ ᴍɪssɪᴏɴ

We arrived back at Aedan's tent early, eager to start. We wanted to be on our way, to give power to this army.

"Luath and my ally, The High King of the Sparrows. Good morning."

"Good morning Aedan, have the eyes of the army returned yet?"

"No, not yet but if I know Donald they will be here shortly."

And right on cue, Donald appeared, eyes dark rimmed and tired.

"What's the situation, Donald?"

"The situation is changing. They were moving north, heading along the west shore of Loch Lomond towards Glen Falloch but they have veered to the west now at Tarbet, and there's only one route they can take now. Glen Croe, Glen Finglas round the head of Loch Fyne to Inverary."

"What else is happening, Donald?"

"Rape, burning, plunder. There's not a man alive between the Fort of the Britons and Tarbet. The women have been violated and the children cry in the heather, the cattle and sheep feed this monster and it moves forward like black fire, not quickly but relentlessly. I have lads heading to Iverary now to warn them to evacuate, head for the hills, burn what will burn and take what can be taken and wait for news from the King."

"You could do no more. Now we must plan. Where are they going, Donald?"

"There are stories of a great fleet to the west, stories that tell of a conquest of the whole western seaboard and Erinn and the northern isles and the land of the Norsemen."

"So where will we stand in their way, where will we stop them meeting their fleet, and Donald my boy, can we do this?"

"We must try, Aedan Bhan. We have warriors who do not know how to lose, but have never tasted victory. We have men that you would not introduce to your sister, but would look after your pet rabbit. We have men who will die with a smile, and men who will die with a frown, for these men have little except their freedom which they all guard jealously. These men would fight each other but you must make them hate and you must hold them together because they can melt away and go home if there is a home. And if there is not a home they will make a home somewhere, anywhere. But, Aedan Bhan they will fight for you if you show them you are as they are. And the place to face our enemy is in the Heartland of the Gael, under Cruachan at the head of Loch Awe and if we do not defeat them there, they will pay dearly for their insolence."

"Donald Campbell, you have fine words for a boy of seventeen and my words are no better. We will face death together at the head of Loch Awe, but we will face death with your brothers and with mine. Luath and my new ally, the High King of the Sparrows, what do you say?"

I spoke for both of us.

"We concur, Aedan Bhan, but we have a little mission to complete before this battle can be fought. How much time do we have Donald?"

"Five days at the most. That army does not move like Highlanders. But it covers the ground and will be approaching Cladich inside five days. You have got to be back before that, otherwise I fear for this Army. And Luath, the Druids tell me the Gods are gathering now."

"Where do they gather, Aedan?"

"Above Cruachan, my friend, above Ben Cruachan."

"Then that is our destination. Come on Tuppence, we have little time, let's go!"

"Luath, look to your safety on that hill, it holds many fears and many dangers. But the blood of Donald an't Sgian will be with you, that I promise. And bring Tuppence back in one piece. I want to tell my grandchildren that I fought shoulder to shoulder with Tuppence Montanus the First, High King of the Sparrows."

"It will be an honour to bring the High King of the Sparrows back safely and with an army beyond your wildest dreams, Donald."

We left Aedan Bhan and Donald in that little tent and headed west through Strath Fillan and Glen Lochy and with Beinn na Sroine on our right a great panorama opened up in front of us.

"What do you think of that, Tuppence?"

"Well, if you let me get my breath back I'll tell you. You've been going like the wind, Luath. Can we stop for a minute or two?"

"Yes, alright, but time is of the essence now."

"Luath, it's beautiful, I've never seen a view like this before. Is this the Heartland that Donald spoke of, and is that Cruachan in the distance and is that Loch Awe?"

"Yes it is the Heartland, yes that is Cruachan and yes that is Loch Awe and yes Tuppence, what a beautiful place to fight, and Donald will make a King one day."

"Where now?"

"Just follow your beak, straight on to Dalmally, it's downhill all the way from here."

ᴛhᴇ BᴀRᴅ

9

We came into the Strath of Orchy and into the settlement at Dalmally, without incident, without hindrance and without trouble, that is until Tuppence said:

"Who's that?"

"Where, Tuppence?"

"Over there, the man waving that big stick above his head."

"Oh my God! Let's go, let's get out of here as quickly as possible."

"Why, Luath, Why?"

"Because I don't want him to see us, that's why."

"Why not?"

"Would you stop saying why, and come on."

"But why?"

"Because he's a danger to every creature in the country."

We got out of sight as quickly as possible, not as quickly as I would have liked but we did get away out of range, then Tuppence started again.

"Who is he Luath and why is he a danger to every creature in the country?"

"Right, we're far enough away now. That…that's Bill."

"Bill? Is that it? Bill what? There must be something else?"

"Bill Spear-Shaker. That big stick he waves above his head is a spear hence the name."

"Bill Spear-Shaker."

"But why is he a danger?"

"Because he's a bard, that's Bill the Bard Spear-Shaker."

"I'm not following this, Luath. What is a bard and why is he dangerous?"

"A bard is a poet, he writes poetry."

"I still don't understand. How can someone who writes poetry be a danger to every creature in the country?"

"He just is, Tuppence, he just is."

"But why?"

"Would you stop saying why all the time?"

"But why, where does he come from?"

"Nobody is really sure where he's from, but the general consensus is that he's from the south."

"How do you know that?"

"Nobody really knows that, but we all figure that's the only direction he could have come from."

"But why, Luath?"

"Is WHY your middle name, Tuppence?"

"No, I'm just interested, and I don't like animals or people being made a fool of. It's just not right, is it?"

"You're right. We think he's from down south because he has a funny accent."

"You are making a fool of him because he has a funny accent. Well I just find that childish. You should be ashamed of yourself. I think that is just pathetic. You should try to have more sympathy, Luath. Sometimes I think you're just a heathen hound. I would like to hear some of his poetry myself."

"No you wouldn't, Tuppence, no you wouldn't."

"Yes I would, Luath, yes I would."

"Right. How can I explain this to you? If you fly at full speed straight into a tree and split your head open, you end up with a nasty wound that takes ages to heal, and when it does heal, you're left with a terrible scar that takes years to go away, if ever."

"Yes, I remember doing that when I was just learning to fly."

"Well, listening to Bill's poetry is like that, only worse. It leaves you scarred for life, but not just superficial scarring. It's deep mental scarring that is almost irreparable."

"He can't be that bad?"

"Look, I've seen grown men weep listening to his poetry."

"Why, because it's so touching?"

"No. It's because his poetry is so bloody awful. But they do say he's become very rich over the years."

"How could he get rich if his poetry is so bad?"

"Well, people pay him to recite his poetry."

"But, if people pay him to recite it, then it has got to be good."

"Not exactly. They pay him to recite his poetry somewhere else, like on the top of a mountain, or on a boat in the middle of a loch, or on that island over there, or like St. Kilda. Locheil once paid him fifty merks to recite one of his poems three quarters of the way up the north face of Ben Nevis in the middle of January, in his underwear. He was hoping to do us all a favour."

"What happened?"

"Bill Spear-Shaker survived."

"I would still like to hear one of his poems."

"You cannot be serious?"

"I am."

"After all I've told you about him."

"Yes, Luath. Can you arrange it?"

"Oh, I can arrange it easily. But are you sure?"

"Yes, positive."

"Alright, on your own head be it."

We retraced our steps to seek out Bill Spear-Shaker. He was easy to find, waving that spear above his head, trying to attract attention. While still some distance away Tuppence said:

"Who are the two girls with Bill, Luath?"

"Oh! They're his daughters."

"And what are their names?"

"Tuppence, do you think we could maybe, if it's alright with you, just get this over and done with pronto. We do have one or two little minor matters to deal with. One springs to mind immediately. It's called a war. There are forty thousand marauding foreigners rampaging about the country, as we speak, or had you forgotten?"

"Oh, no Luath, I haven't forgotten, but surely they can wait ten minutes till I listen to a poem?"

"Well, would you like to listen quickly, so we can move along?"

"Oh, yes, Luath, I'll do that."

"Thank you, Tuppence."

"Don't mention it."

"What are the girls names?"

"I don't think you want to know that. It gets complicated."

"Oh, yes I do."

"I was afraid of that. Well the one on the right is called Bob."

"Isn't Bob a boy's name? Why would anybody call their daughter Bob?"

"Bob is a boy's name, Tuppence, I think Bill was hoping for a son, so he called her Bob, simple as that."

"They are very bonny girls. So what's the one on the left called."

"Well, she's called boB backwards."

"What!"

"boB backwards."

"Am I missing something here, is that not just the same name only the other way round?"

"I don't think it's you that's missing something. I have a strange feeling that maybe Bill has empty space somewhere."

"Do you know why he did it?"

"Well, I told you he was hoping for a son, but he got a daughter instead, well he didn't just get one daughter he got two at the same time, identical twins. So Bill gave them identical names but by giving them the same name he couldn't tell them apart so to solve the problem he spelt one of their names backwards in order to distinguish them."

"But, Luath that doesn't work, does it, how does that work? Does it work, what's going on, and oh, it's beginning to hurt, Luath."

"Lets leave that there for the time being, Tuppence. You're starting to move into brain burnout and meltdown mode. I told you Bill had a certain effect on everyone he comes into contact with, and you haven't even met him yet."

"Are you sure you want to go ahead with this poetry business now?"

"Er…well…yes and no…"

"What do you mean yes and no? It's either yes or no. Which is it to be?"

"Yes, let's go for a yes, it's bound to be different isn't it?"

"There's nothing surer than that. It might well give you a little insight into the workings of the mind of a geni…I was going to say genius but there must be another word, what about cretin, yes that's more like it."

"What's a cretin?"

"Well, Tuppence you're just about to find out, in fact you are going to get a ringside seat, a hands-on experience, a practical demonstration from a master and if you don't learn something from this, I'll be most disappointed in you."

"Oh, I will."

"Are you ready? You wouldn't like to say a little prayer or something first?"

"No, Luath I'm fine."

We approached Bill the Bard Spear-Shaker with more than a little trepidation.

"Good morning, Bill."

"Ah, Luath, Good morning to you and how are you this sun-kissed morn?"

"I'm just fine Bill. Can I introduce you to a very good friend of mine? This is Tuppence Why Montanus."

"Good morning, Tuppence Why Montanus, good morning. Any friend of Luath's is a friend of swine. May I introduce you to my two beautiful sonters, this is Bob on my left and this is boB backwards on my right."

"How do you do, Bob and how do you do boB, I am very pleased to meet you. I've heard a lot about you. My friend Luath has told me about you. You must be very proud of your father – the best bard in the Highlands."

"How are you Tuppence Why Montanus? We are pleased to meet you."

"Luath, my friend, what can I do for you? It's so long since I've seen you. What can I do for you both?"

"Nothing for me Bill, but Tuppence would like to hear one of your poems."

"Oh! This is indeed an unexpected pleasure, Tuppence. Which one of my latest masterpieces would you like to hear?"

"I'm sorry Bill, but I'm not from these parts and I've never heard any of your poems before. Maybe you could tell me what poems are available to hear."

"Surely, Tuppence, I have a range of poems and plays to suit every taste from the simple to the incredibly mundane, just stop me when I get to one you think you might like to hear. I could recite 'The Amazing World of Flat Worms' which is very popular with the underground movement, or 'Hold it, that's my Chicken Mister', which goes down a bomb in O'Donnell's chicken burger restaurants, which are all over the Emerald Isle. Or I could recite 'I'm a Bit Early for a very Unimportant Appointment'. But my latest and I think one of the greatest is 'The Legend of Cannibal Hector MacPhee.'"

"I think I would like to hear 'The Legend of Cannibal Hector MacPhee'."

"Would you like to hear it in the Gaelic or English or in Latin or Greek or in Hindi or Faeroese?"

"What do you think, Luath? I'm not really sure."

"I think you should maybe stick with English, Tuppence, as it's the only one you understand. What do you think?"

"Alright, I'll go with that. English please, Bill."

I tried to dull the pain a little by suggesting the abridged English version.

"Just before you start, Bill I'm going to have to leave now. I've a very important date. I'm going to leave you four together. I'll be back for you later and I'll bring a psychiatrist with me, Tuppence. Bye now."

"Right, Tuppence I'll begin. Are you alright there Bob and boB?"

"Yes." "Yes."

"Tuppence Why Montanus, This is for you. The Legend of Cannibal Hector MacPhee. Abridged English version, the first ten verses."

"Excuse me, Bill, I would like to know how many verses the unabridged English version has, please?"

"About eighty."

"Ten will be fine, I've got a war to deal with, and I don't have a lot of time. Luath said I've got to listen quickly, so if you can hurry it along a bit I'd much appreciate it."

"Righty oh then, Tuppence. Here we go!"

THE LEGEND OF CANNIBAL HECTOR MacPHEE

It's Cannibal Hector MacPhee,
Half hidden behind that old tree,
His motive is clear,
He's after a beer,
And something tasty for tea.
He's a giant of a man,
About twenty-three hands,
He's callous and brutal and mean.
If you see him near, make sure you get clear,
Or it's the last you'll ever be seen.
Abandoned aged three on the Isle of Tiree,
Young Hector had quite a bad start,
But in not very long,
He grew taller and strong,
On a diet of liver and heart.
He left his fair isle,
And went to Argyll,
Where the pickings were richer by far,
And after a while he was living in style,
And even bought a wee car.
His fame it did spread,

As far as the Med,
Where the people all trembled with fright,
And on an isle over there, he strangled a bear,
And then went after a fight.
Now MacPhee liked a dram,
Like the rest of the clan,
But too much drink made him dizzy,
And another strange thing about drinking the gin,
It made Hector MacPhee's pee fizzy.
Now this fizzy pee, sure it baffled MacPhee,
And he wasn't so sure how to tell it,
To the man from The Board,
Who said, Oh! My good Lord,
Why don't you bottle it, can it, and sell it.
MacPhee scratched his head,
As he lay in his bed,
To ponder this business proposal,
It's all very fine it's like bottling wine.
But how much "P" is at my disposal?
Now this brute of a man
Who would eat your right hand
Was not sure in which way to veer,
He decided at last to give up his past,
And change the direction of his career.
He had made a few bob,
From his previous job,
As a slayer of homo-sap-iens,
But from this moment on his old life was gone,
Now his aim was to please human-be-ings.

THE END by Bill the Bard Spear-Shaker

"There you go, Tuppence my little chicken. What did you think of that? Isn't that just the most remarkable poem in the English language? Or any language, I am particularly pleased with the way I managed to get it to rhyme and that wasn't easy I can tell you, that was the really difficult bit. The rest of it just seems to flow like a river of broken glass. That's real poetry, none of your pseudo-intellectual rubbish here, none of that nonsense about wandering about up to your armpits in daffodils, this is real stuff, straight from the heart, unbridled genius."

"Bill, could you help me up please?"

"Certainly, Tuppence there you go."

"I feel a wee bit dizzy, could I have a drink of water, please?"

"boB fetch Tuppence some water."

"Well, Tuppence what did you think of it?"

"I've never actually heard anything like it in my life, Bill, it's absolutely unique. I find it very difficult to express in words exactly what I'm feeling at the moment. Maybe through time I will understand and come to terms with the enormity and magnitude of the intellectual battering that I have just received at the hands of a master."

"Thank you indeed Tuppence Why Montanus, I knew you'd like it, I just knew. I had a feeling when we meet that you had a similar if slightly less elevated intellect than myself. You and I are intellectual giants, we should do this more often."

"There's Luath now. Over here, Luath, over here!"

"Well, how are you all getting along, Bill?"

"Tuppence was just telling us how much he'd enjoyed the recital, Luath, you can bring your little friend back anytime."

"That's just fine, Bill."

"Luath, Luath, could you take me to war now, please. I would really like to go to war now, please. Please, Luath take me somewhere safe."

"We'd better get going, Bill, affairs of state don't you know. Bye Bill, bye Bob, bye boB. See you again sometime soon."

"Goodbye, my little chicken. Goodbye Tuppence. Goodbye Tuppence."

We left quickly. I had an extraordinary feeling that Tuppence wanted to get out the vicinity in a hurry. I'm sure the option of leaving the country had crossed his mind as well. Tuppence didn't speak for a while.

CRUACHAN

"Tuppence, how do you feel now?"

"A wee bit shaky, Luath."

"Well it's your own fault you silly little sparrow. I told you it's unhealthy to be in Bill's company. Anyway let's get going or we'll be late for the battle."

"They wouldn't start without us, would they?"

"The way you're going, the whole war will be over before we reach Cruachan."

"Luath, I'm sorry, I've just never been in a position like this before."

"Do not apologise, Tuppence. That is a sign of weakness."

"Maybe I am weak, maybe I'm not cut out for this, maybe I should not be here and maybe you should go to Hell, Luath."

"That's better, Tuppence, my little warrior, my little chicken."

"Don't call me a chicken, and especially not my little chicken!"

"In that case, Tuppence, just get a grip of yourself. Just exactly what do you think we are doing here? This is not a little bedtime story, you can't hide under the covers here. This is bloody war, this is going to test the nerve of the bravest heart and I am not going to lose you in this. I am not going to lose you so you will now become like me and you're going to hate yourself for a time and you're going to survive and we will maybe go home together, if you'll permit me."

"I think you like me, Luath."

"Let us go to Cruachan and gain what we can for these men, the men that Kings rely on, the men that give everything and ask for nothing but food and maybe a dram."

We rounded the head of Loch Awe and started to climb, looking for the summit. But Cruachan is no ordinary mountain. There must be six or seven peaks and we had no idea which one to approach, but we moved forward and upwards. We passed Monadh Driseig and Beinn a Bhuridh, then set our sights on Stob Daimh and saw nothing. Our eyes then turned to Meall Cuanail. We headed there, then we heard, then we saw, then we were scared.

"I don't think I like the sound of this, Luath."

"It's alright, it's just the Gods talking."

"They talk quite loud, don't they? It sounds to me like a thunder storm."

"That, Tuppence is a conversation, nothing more, nothing less."

"And who converses at that decibel level, may I ask?"

"There can only be two who talk like this, only two."

"Who are they then?"

"Thor, Norse God of thunder and Tarvos Taranos the Celtic God of thunder and God of the bulls."

We moved toward the storm then something strange happened as we crossed Drochaid Ghlas (the Grey Bridge), and approached Coire Caorach (the Corrie of the Sheep). We saw something that should not be here.

"Tuppence what do you see?"

"Trees."

"That's exactly what I see, but this is not possible. The tree line finishes fifteen hundred feet below us but these trees block our path to the summit. There would appear to be no way round. What do you think my friend?"

"I can fly over them."

"Yes, you can but I cannot. I have a feeling that we are going to be tested on this hill."

"Luath, with every breath I take in this world I am being tested, but you said yourself we are immoral, we cannot die, there is only one way for us and that is forward, through the trees and upward."

"Immortal, you dope! But you're right, we have no option, let's press on through the trees to The Gods."

There was fear in my heart as we approached this wood and when we entered, the hairs on the back of my neck were bristling, Tuppence flew in as if he was going to a party. Oh! For a pure heart and a clear conscience.

The wood was dense, the undergrowth was thick and we had crossed another line. This was not Cruachan. This felt alien. We were not in Alba now, but we moved ever forward, ever upward. An eternity had passed when we came upon a clearing, a clearing, almost level, almost circular with the most luxuriant grass you have ever seen. It was at least a hundred yards across, and it looked like a theatre – a place where plays were performed, or games were played. The air was warm and humid. This was not three thousand feet up on Cruachan in May. This was somewhere else.

"Tuppence, be vigilant and listen, we must cross this space in order to proceed and talk to The Gods."

"I don't see a problem, Luath. What a beautiful place! This must be what I've heard some people call Heaven."

"Yes, this is most probably Heaven, like Orlando in Florida with alligators and flies and Walt Disney. You'd like that wouldn't you?"

"Oh, yes, can we go there sometime. Please?"

"Let's get through this little situation first, what do you say?"

"OK, Luath, but I'd like to go to Disneyland."

"Right, one day we'll go there."

Now I was reluctant to move forward across the clearing. My first instinct was to sprint but I held back, because there was no sound, no hint of noise, no real hint of trouble, so we moved out slowly in a straight line heading for the nearest cover possible. A third of the way across things kind of changed.

"Luath, what's that noise?"

"What noise?"

"That noise, the noise behind us. Sometimes I think you're getting a bit deaf."

"Could you be more specific, Tuppence?"

"Well it sounds like a herd of buffalo coming through the trees."

No buffalo appeared, but to my horror the undergrowth burst apart and the biggest wild boar in the universe came charging towards me at full throttle, huge tusks curled over an enormous snout. He did seem to look just a touch ANGRY.

"Run, Luath!"

I took off as fast as I could, but with every stride he was gaining ground.

"Put the foot down, Luath! Run, he's catching you!"

It all happened so quickly, but it was like slow motion. I could now feel the hot breath of this snorting monster on my rear, Tuppence was screaming my name and I felt I had just seconds before impact. My speed, I feared would not be enough on this occasion. Then in front, three figures appeared out of the wood – I was heading straight for them, I couldn't focus on them, but I could see they were armed and I saw spears raised in their hands. This is it. I had been so easily trapped. Now I was going to shed blood on the tusks of a wild boar or on the cold steel of a spear point. Tuppence forgive me my little friend. I saw then, two spears leave the hands of these dark men in front, I could see the steel glint as these weapons rotated on their deadly journey, then I heard the spears whisper, but they did not strike, they whispered death as they passed. They missed me! Thanks to the Gods! Then I heard two sounds together, I heard steel slamming into hair and flesh and bone, and heard an almighty squeal that echoed throughout the forest, then the ground shook, and shook. I staggered and slid and collapsed in a heap at the feet of these dark men.

"Good day to you, Luath and good day to you, Tuppence."

"What?"

"Good day."

"You have the advantage over us, Sir. You know our names but we do not know yours."

"Allow me to do the introductions. We share the blood of Donald an't Sgian, my name is Black Dan Campbell of Strachur and these are my brothers Eion and Iain. Donald is our cousin."

"Forgive me for being so abrupt, Dan, But I thought the spears were for me, I owe you my life, I will be in your debt for ever, thank you."

"Och, it was nothing at all, I thought you were starting to pull away from that old boar anyway."

"I wasn't convinced Dan. Still, Donald seems to be true to his word, Tuppence."

"Yes, Luath, but you did look a bit slow today, your pick up wasn't as sharp as normal."

"Thank you very much. I can rely on you to boost the old ego when it's flagging."

"That's OK, Luath."

"One thing does concern me slightly, Dan."

"What's that?"

"It was yourself and Eion who threw your weapons?"

"Yes, that's right."

"Now the boar was directly behind me and you were directly in front of me and I was going slightly uphill, how much of the boar could you see?"

"Not a lot."

"So what did you aim at, Dan?"

"I aimed at your left eye. I kind of figured the speed you were going you'd be well past the sharp bit before it struck home."

"And you, Eoin?"

"I aimed at your right eye. I had similar thoughts, but I thought my spear point had a chance of going through the flappy bit of your ear before it struck home."

"That's what I was afraid of. Have either of you ever missed before?"

"Never, not once in thirty years that I can remember, but the memory's kind of going. Can you remember missing, at any time Eoin?"

"No. What would be the bloody point in that? That's just bloody stupid and bloody dangerous and we'd go bloody hungry. Anyway, which one of these spears is yours Dan? Mine has my name on it, but the lettering is getting so small, I just can't read it any more."

"Very amusing, Eoin Campbell, I'll remember that."

"Ha, ha, och, that's a good one, Eoin, isn't it, Luath? He's a funny man, I like him. But he does swear a lot, Luath, doesn't he? That's not good, is it, all that swearing, it's not nice, is it, Luath, but he is funny, isn't he, Luath?"

"It's alright, Tuppence, calm down, your mother's not here at the moment, you're allowed to laugh and I'm sure, Eoin wouldn't swear in front of your mother, would you, Eoin?"

"No, never, not in front of a woman, I draw the line there, I've never sworn in front of a female of any description, anywhere, at any time, in my bloody life."

"Anyway you boys are as handy with steel as your cousin, Donald."

"And who do you think taught Donald? But that's a story for another time. Luath I think we have a slight problem here."

"Problem?"

"This place is not real, it should not be here. There should be no trees here and it should not be warm here. My brothers and I have been on this hill since we were little boys and we have never been here before. This place does not exist. It's an illusion."

"Was that boar an illusion Dan Campbell?"

"No, he was real, he was as real as the steel that stopped him breathing, but that old boar was not chasing you, he was fleeing from something. All you did was get in his way. You were in the wrong place at the right time."

"So, what frightened him?"

"I'm not sure but he's dead now and can't tell us. I'll gralloch the old fellow now and hang him up, he'll be ready for eating in a week or so."

"Luath."

"Yes, Tuppence."

"I don't feel very well."

"You'll be fine, my little friend. It will be better than salt herring, and a pleasant change from the venison you're used to Dan. Is that not right?"

"Absolutely, Luath, a real pleasant change and there's plenty of him."

BLACK AND WHITE

"Luath, can I speak with you alone for a couple of minutes?"

"Certainly, Dan, let's walk."

"There's something seriously wrong here. This place does not exist. It's almost like a theatre. Something is going to be enacted here that is not good for us and I do not like it."

"I feel the same, but what can we do?"

"I'm not sure, but this smells like a trap, it looks like a killing field to me. What better place to destroy your enemy, I couldn't find a better spot myself. That old boar was not our problem I fear. He was just frightened, but frightened of what? There could be a clue in something we saw today, which was unusual, to say the least."

"What did you see?"

"Well, Donald's words came quickly to our ears and we were on the hill before you today and we watched as you found your way and we stayed close, but behind you we did see something. I think there were two."

"Two what, Dan?"

"That's what I don't know and that is what worries me, Luath. I know every creature in these hills but I've never seen before what I saw today, I do not think they are of this world."

"What did they look like? Dan, I need to know, I need to know what we face. Were they human or beasts?"

"They looked human and they looked like beasts."

"That's not a great deal of help."

"I know. One was tall and reasonably straight and walked on two legs or it looked like two legs, but he was out of proportion. From that distance he looked crippled, disfigured and was dressed in light coloured clothing and seemed to wear a hood."

"What was the other one like?"

"Different but the same."

"Different but the same?"

"Yes, the same feeling emanated from them both, but this one was dark and low and crippled and disfigured and I don't know if it had legs or not. It seemed to slide over the ground like a fish and it also had a hood."

"I have heard of creatures like this before, creatures from the future. They call them clones, creatures from a different place, creatures with certain powers."

"What is a clone?"

"Well, in the future people will try to act like Gods and scientists will take parts of a human and make other humans from these pieces and these new humans will be exactly the same as the ones they took the parts from, or so they thought."

"I don't really see a problem there, Luath."

"There's no problem except they didn't realise that human beings are not perfect and in their genes lie all the slime and filth of generation upon generation of greed and jealousy and bigotry and deformity and hate and lies and let's face it, Dan, human beings are the most despicable creatures that have ever roamed this planet."

"I couldn't agree with you more, Luath, in fact a cull might be necessary and I'm all for that and I have a couple of brothers who will help."

"Thank you, Dan, I'll let you know. Anyway, after a few years these little defects emerge in this cloning process, and I think we have clones around us now and I think they are advanced into the process of degeneration and that is when they are dangerous. We must fight this evil with our mightiest weapons."

Then it started to rain and the wind blew and we went back to the others. We were in the middle of this green circle surrounded by trees, and Tuppence came to me and said:

"Luath, it's raining."

"I know my little friend, I know it's raining."

"Luath its raining blood."

"I know its raining blood."

"Luath, this is not good, and the wind blows and its getting dark and I'm really scared and it's still warm and sticky, what can we do?"

"Tuppence, we have a night ahead that will test our mettle, but these men with us are descendants of Pharaohs and do not fear anything but themselves. We are in the hands of men that trust no one, bow to no one, care for no one, man or God, and will not be wanting when the time is upon us."

Lights appeared, strange lights, lights within darkness on our intended path, then two figures came out of the gloom, the creatures Dan had spoken of. They were hideous, almost as Dan had described, but in close up it was difficult to believe their deformities and they came to the edge of the wood and showed themselves and spoke, and they spoke with voices from the depths of depravity and despair and the smell of them was the smell of desolation and decay.

We moved forward to meet them, Campbell steel at our head.

"Who do you wish to speak with?" Eoin said in an elegant manner.

"I will speak with the dog," the white one said, saliva dripping from its mouth.

"This is not a dog, you slavering bastard, this is Luath, the Hound of Aedan Bhan, High King of the Albannach and if I permit you, and if he is willing, you may speak."

"Eoin, go easy, till I find out exactly what this is all about, just hang fire."

"Give me the word and I'll smoke these bastards over a fire tonight."

"Hold on to your temper, just a wee bit longer, Eoin, just a bit, I'll tell you when."

I turned to the creatures.

"If you wish to speak to me, I require your name."

"I am called Ammac-an-Geal."

"And your companion, what is his name?"

"This is my brother and he is named Ammac-an-Dubh."

"Your names are unfamiliar. Where are you from?"

"We are the future and we come to help you all."

"But you block our path. We have a mission and we will not be dissuaded."

"Your mission is doomed, you cannot resist, we are the future. Your Gods are dead, they have no place in this world now, we will lead you to a land of peace and freedom and plenty."

"And will we all look like you in this land of peace and freedom and plenty?"

"You mock us dog. We are here to help."

"I do not mock you, Ammac-an-Geal and I do not mock your brother Ammac-an-Dubh, but if you are the future, the Gods will surely help us and if you have the remotest link with the Army of the White Dragon, we are enemies for all of eternity and you should leave now, while you can and if you leave now you might retain your breath, although it smells like the urine of the cat and when we deal with you it will be in my time and in my space and you will be treated with contempt and disdain and your miserable bodies will be dismembered and burnt in the fires of Hades and you will remain there in eternal suffering, until we call an end."

Eoin whispered: "Slightly heavy, Luath, but good."

"You will not leave this place alive dog, and your feathered friend will not make the journey you desire. We have drawn a circle that you cannot break through. You will die here with your Campbell guard."

I could feel my Campbell guard tense at that insult and I feared blood would be spilt too early on this journey.

But as Ammac-an-Geal spoke, the hand of Iain Campbell touched my neck and pointed skywards. Above us in the gloom circled a bird. Iain whispered:

"It's a Hoodie."

We kept silent then and listened and waited.

"My brother Ammac-an-Geal speaks the truth, you will not defeat us here in this circle and your lives will now be short. Your Gods are dead."

Without speaking we moved backwards slowly one pace at a time. As we moved backwards they came forward further into the circle, Ammac-an-Geal shuffling and stumbling, Ammac-an-Dubh almost sliding over the ground, arms assisting almost useless legs. How did these creatures ever come to be here? They should have been slaughtered for their looks alone. 'Hideous' is a word of beauty compared to these.

They began to speak simultaneously, then to roar at us and threaten us and threaten each other, and then they came to blows, striking each other with grotesque limbs. My little band of brothers held their nerve and watched and continued to retreat slowly.

Then she struck with awesome speed and power. Ammac-an-Geal had raised his right arm to deal his brother another blow and as he looked skywards, she swept down and ripped into his face, wing feathers flailing and locked her talons so deep into the flesh of his cheeks that we heard her claws screech on the bone of his skull and then like lighting she tore his left eye out of it's socket and burst it like a balloon with her great black beak. The eye dangled and he bled ferociously, screaming and wailing.

"One eye will be sufficient for today," she said as she circled round us, flesh and blood dripping from her beak and claws. "We are not dead yet, we live in your hearts and minds and we look forward to speaking with you, Tuppence, when you reach us."

And with that she swept towards the heavens. Ammac-an-Geal and his brother beat a hasty retreat, shuffling and stumbling and colliding with one another back into the safety of the wood they thought was impregnable, still lamenting in pain and anguish and humiliation.

"Luath, the hooded crow, who was she and how did she know my name?"

"She, my friend, is the Queen of the Gods, and when she comes to earth she is called Corvus Corone Cornix and she puts on her feathers of black and grey, and she sharpens her talons and she sharpens her beak, and that's why you should never do harm to a hooded crow."

"She looks like she can take care of herself. What do you say, Dan?"

"I think you have a point there, Tuppence. She certainly has several points of her own and has shown us also that these two creatures bleed and feel pain."

"It's stopped raining, Luath."

"I think we should rest now. Tomorrow could be pretty ugly, but I don't think we'll hear from the brothers tonight. But we'll post a guard just in case."

We rested well and took our turn on guard duty. Eoin woke me at daylight.

"Luath, look at this."

"It's away, Eoin, the circle, it's gone. What do you make of that, Iain?"

"Now their names begin to make more sense. It is becoming much clearer to me. I think they thought their task would be easy amongst the men of the north, but I think also they will be back to haunt us until battle is joined and they will be stung by our hooded crow and we must destroy them and cut them into pieces and burn the remnants in the fire that consumes all and cleanses."

Iain Campbell spoke little, but when he spoke, we listened.

ᴄhe ᴄαϻpbᴇʟʟ ɢuαrᴅ

"Well, for the time being our path is clear and we know our route. Do we have the company of the Campbell guard for the rest of the journey or not? What do you think, Tuppence?"

"I don't think Tuppence need answer that question, Luath. I, Black Dan Campbell, am the head of this family, and my brothers and I will be with you till this battle is concluded, victory or defeat, right or wrong, but we alone will burn the black and the white."

"Is that the answer you expected, Tuppence?"

"No, Luath, I expected them to run away."

These three brothers laughed with us at that little moment in time and I just hoped we would laugh together again, when this was all over. There are no certainties in this world and the Gods that smile on you today may not tomorrow.

I think I have neglected my duty to describe my companions to you. You know Tuppence by now. He is a sparrow and he's stupid and dull in the head and has a serious problem with gravity and flying and all the things that sparrows do but he's my little friend and I think I maybe like him and sometimes not and sometimes certainly not. But it would not be the same if he wasn't here, though it could well be better.

Tuppence and I have companions that I did not choose and have no control over, but they are here and they make things happen and when things happen, then you know you are alive and things will be different. You can learn a lot about people in a few hours sometimes, and you will learn what we learn as we journey with our Campbell guard.

Black Dan Campbell, not a big man, maybe five foot seven, with the look of Spain in him, black haired, black bearded as tough as teak and the same colour, agile in mind and body, carries a host of weaponry on and about and concealed in his Highland clothing, expert with every one, history and learning run through his veins, a man of the west and he carries a temper.

Eion Neil Campbell, bigger, six foot one, Campbell coloured, fair skin weather-beaten, red-fair hair, powerful, muscular, alert, teller of stories, full of mischief, swears a little, talks a lot, knows what the fox will do before the fox has made up its mind, more places to conceal weapons than Black Dan and carries more, knows how to use every one of them, known in more places than the Devil and he carries a temper.

Iain Donald Campbell, five foot eleven, fair haired, fair skinned, broad, strong, deep, silent, reliable, knows what the other two know but doesn't talk about it, thinks before he utters a word; if you were to build an army, this is your cornerstone; courage is his mistress, carries his fair share of weapons, don't stand in front of him and never behind and whatever you do don't make him angry, he carries a TEMPER.

These then are our companions, at least for the next few days. We do not always feel safe in their company but we console ourselves with the fact that anything we meet be it man or animal or demon will be a lot less safe than we are, facing this Campbell guard.

ᴄhe ᴀppoinᴄᴍenᴄ

"There's the summit," Dan shouted. "Straight ahead, we'll be there in half an hour. Isn't she beautiful, the peak of Ben Cruachan! It felt like the top of the world, with views that some people would die for, and have. Tuppence asked:

"What do we do now, Luath?"

"Ah... not sure."

"What do you mean, you're not sure? You brought us here."

"I've never done this before. It's not often one has an appointment with the Gods, don't you know. It's not as if we can just knock on the door, or ring the bell."

"OK, so what do we do?"

"I think we'll just wait, something will happen."

"Dan, what do you think?"

"I think, Luath's right, if we wait, it'll happen."

"Eoin, what about you?"

"I think we should wait."

"Iain, what do you think we should do?"

"Wait."

But that wasn't good enough for Tuppence.

"I've risked life and limb to get here, faced untold dangers, sweated in the jungle, dreamed of Disneyland, been rained upon by blood, seen the two nastiest creatures in the universe, been mentally assaulted by some raving lunatic of a poet and I am now freezing my a...a...a... feet off on the top of this big lump of a mountain and all you lot want to do is laze about and wait. Well I think you all just a bunch of w...w...w... wets, that's what I think."

"Tell us about the poet, Tuppence, we haven't heard that one yet, that sounds intriguing."

"No, Dan, it's too embarrassing, too fresh in the memory."

"I'll tell the boys."

"No you won't, Luath, don't you dare!"

"I think you should maybe rest, my little warrior, I think you should lie down for a while."

"Why are you being nice to me, Luath? What's this all about?"

"I just think you should relax."

"Why? There's something going on here."

"Don't be daft, Tuppence, it's just that the on the next little bit of our quest, you're on your own."

"What do you mean, on my own?"

"Well just what I say, you're on your own."

"Oh, so you're going to leave me on my own, on top of this big hill and go away."

"No Tuppence, we'll still be here on top of this big hill, it's just that you'll be somewhere else."

"What do you mean, somewhere else?"

"Well you have to meet the Gods. You are my messenger with wings."

"And where will I be, Luath?"

"Up there."

"What do you mean, up there?"

"Just what I say, up there."

"You mean you want me to jump off this mountain. Don't be daft, Luath, I've never been at three and a half thousand feet before and you know fine I'm scared of heights."

"You're a bird, are you not, Tuppence?"

"Yes, I'm a bird, but I'm a low level sort of a bird. Thirty feet, maybe thirty five, after forty feet I just get nauseous and black out."

"Maybe I picked the wrong bird. I'm sorry, if you're not cut out for this sort of thing, we may as well go home now. Let us all go now! I'm terribly sorry about this folks, that's the end of the book. Bye now."

"Now hold on a minute, Luath, I'm in this book as well, you can't just cut me out like that."

"Why not, my little chicken?"

"Don't call me that, you big dog, you big stupid DOG, I'm the star of this production."

"Oh! Is that right now? You're so short you wouldn't get a part in Braveheart."

"Braveheart? Never heard of her."

Iain spoke: "The show's over, Luath. Is your little friend ready? I dearly hope so because here they come."

They came in with thunder and lightning and all the things that Gods do well and I felt sore for my little friend and I said to him:

"Tuppence, can you do this? For if you cannot, I will understand and I'll take you out of this place."

"Do you think that I have come here to fail you, Luath?"

"No, never."

"Then what do I do?"

"Just follow the Queen. You know her already."

Ben Cruachan shook, the world shook, our lives trembled and the hooded crow descended in a spiral from out of that storm and took my little companion into the unknown and I was not happy.

"Right, boys, come on, let's shelter from the storm. Come on, Luath, you'll get soaked in this, come on, he'll be alright, he'll be back before you know it. There's a fine spot over here."

Dan's words were kind, but I followed reluctantly, my mind was on higher things, how much higher I did not know, but I did know that this would be a trial.

Dan had found the best shelter possible under the circumstances, a collection of huge rocks with sufficient overhang to keep the worst of the rain off us; the wind came mostly at us from behind. We settled down as best we could to watch and wait. A few minutes ago this was the most beautiful place in the world, now it was a raging hell, with thunder rolling round our heads and lightning striking the rocks that gave us shelter. The mist went this way and that and the rain came from every conceivable direction. But our own safety played little on our minds.

"Do you think Tuppence can survive this onslaught, Luath?" said Eoin, with obvious concern.

"That I do not know, that I dearly wish to know, for the answer will determine certain other things."

"What things?" they said in unison.

"I promised him once, that if anything should happen to him in this world, that I would share his fate."

There was a long silence.

Then a hand touched my shoulder and Dan said.

"You are as we three are, you are indeed brothers."

"I think you've answered some other questions too," said Eion.

"What questions?"

"We all knew you needed wings for your mission, and we all had our own ideas as to what your companion would be. Luath will bring the mighty golden Eagle, no, Luath will bring the Osprey, no, Luath will bring the blackest Raven, but no, Luath you brought a Sparrow."

"Are you taking the mickey, Eion Campbell?"

"Yes I am."

"Good. I'm glad."

We all laughed for the first time in hours. Then Dan roared: "Is this bloody thing never going to stop?"

And then as quickly as it had begun, it stopped, just like that and the day was fine again and standing right in front of us was Tuppence.

"Tuppence! Are you alright?"

"Who me, yes I'm fine, but why are you all wet?"

"Because it's been raining for the last three hours. In fact you dozy bird, it just hasn't been raining it's been the worst storm this century and we've been out in it, waiting for you. But hang on, Tuppence you're dry. How did you manage to stay dry?"

"It wasn't raining where I was, in fact it was absolutely beautiful where I was."

"What about the storm then?"

"Oh! That's just one of those things to impress you mortals, they just do it for show, it's sort of PR stuff."

"What do you mean PR stuff?"

"Public relations."

"I know what PR stands for, you dope, I just wanted to know why?"

"Well, they have a reputation to uphold, they couldn't arrive on the back of a milk float, could they now, that wouldn't be very impressive now would it?"

"That's true enough. How did it go with you amongst the Gods?"

"Come on, Tuppence, how did you get on?"

Three dripping wet Campbells were as anxious as I was to hear what had transpired.

"Fine."

"Is that it? Fine! Come on tell us, what was the place like?"

"I can't tell you that."

"Why not?"

"I'm under oath."

"You don't know what 'under oath' means."

"I know I don't but I'm under one just the same. I have promised not to tell a living soul what it was like there."

"Alright then, who did you see and who did to you talk to?"

"Oh I can tell you that."

"What are they like, the Gods?"

"Very much like human beings, but with one glaring difference."

"What's the difference?"

"The Gods are intelligent."

That brought a snigger from those present.

ᴄhe ʀɪᴆᴆʟᴇ

"I saw many Gods and talked to many, like Alcis and Bragi and Thor and Odin. I saw Danu and the Tuatha de Danann, Tarvos Taranos and the Lord of the Ravens.

But I think we should be on our way because we have a couple of more things to do before we can approach this battle."

"Have the Gods told you what to do, Tuppence?"

"We have two tasks to perform before we can return to Aedan Bhan."

"What are they my little friend?"

Dan, Eoin, Iain and I all held our breath for we all knew that what the Gods ask is not always possible.

"Firstly, we must find a wise man and secondly we must gather some stones."

There were sighs all round.

"Thank goodness for that," said Dan. "For one horrible moment I thought they were going to make it tough for us, this sounds very reasonable, I was getting a bit nervous."

"Tuppence, what's that tied round your left leg?"

"Oh, that's a silver thread from Danu."

"And what's it for?"

"For the stones."

There was silence for a moment or two while this sunk in. Then Eion said. "I take it then these stones have got holes in them, like beads?"

"Yes, that's right, Eion."

"And where do we find these stones?"

"I don't know."

"And how do we find out, where to find the stones?"

"The wise man will tell us."

"And where is the wise man?"

"I don't know."

"Still quite happy about this situation, Dan?" asked Eoin.

"Point taken, Eoin, but there must be more information, Tuppence?"

"Oh yes. I have a little story which will help us find the wise man."

"See, Eoin, you've got to ask the right questions."

"Little story, Dan, you know fine what this is going to be, don't you? It's going to be a riddle isn't it, a bloody riddle and how good are you at bloody riddles, how good am I at riddles and what about Iain – can he solve riddles – no."

"Go ahead, Tuppence, tell us the story."

"Alright, Dan, here we go."

So Tuppence told us:

Under your feet lies a space in the ground
It is full of volumes that were lost, now are found
And far to East, where the Gypsies are from
Came a man with three ships and a dream and a song.
His hands and his face, they are scarred by a fire
Undeniable, wise man, never a liar
He holds all the truths that the ancients knew well
Be friends with this man, you are under his spell.
He will tell you the way and the path and the means
He will tell you impossible, just but a dream,
But if you hold a key that he wants and desires

He will show you the way to content your own ires,
The treasures he keeps they may win you a battle
But to speak to this man you must look to his cattle
They drink in the fresh and they bathe in the brine
And there's nothing in here that you'll say is mine.
The key to his door, it is hard to describe
It's not big, it's not little, but it is at low tide
There are rocks, there are gulls, it's a frightening place
And if it's early you are, you could lose the race.
But inside it's so warm and so bright and much cleaner
Than the place that you left when life was much meaner,
It's a room, it's a hall, an incredible court
Why not sit back, relax and enjoy a fine port.
He has scholars and scribes and artists and minions
Reserve your ideas and your opinions,
There are warriors there that would put you to shame,
Joining them now would enhance all our fame.

"Is that it? "

"Yes, that it."

"Well what do you think of that little lot, Dan? Pretty straight forward, Eh! Shouldn't take us more than, what, two or three weeks to solve this simple little puzzle. I personally thought they would have made it a lot more difficult. Yes, I think the Gods are being rather lenient on us, I was looking for a real tester."

"Och, shut up, Eoin. It's not my fault it's a riddle. At fist glance it seems rather complicated, but at the second glance things become much clearer. Yes, at second glance it looks impossible."

"Come on, Dan, You're the head of this family and you're supposed to be the intelligent one, you should be able to do things like this."

This was getting us nowhere rapidly. I had to step in there.

"Right, lads, that's enough. Until we solve this riddle we cannot move forward and we certainly cannot move backwards, and we just can't return to Aedan Bhan empty handed. The language used is not difficult, we must solve this and quickly. Let's look at it one verse at a time. Surely we can get enough out of it to move forward. What do you say?"

"You're absolutely right. Let's break it down piece by piece. We'll get something out of this riddle. There's got to be enough brain power among the five of us, surely."

Thank goodness for Iain Campbell.

"Right, let's have a go."

Under your feet lies a space in the ground

"What does that mean? Well if we take it literally there's a hole in the ground under our feet inside Ben Cruachan. Everyone happy with that?"

One or two groans of approval.

It is, full of volumes, that were lost, now are found

"Volumes, Anyone have an answer to that?"

"Books."

"OK, books. So, what have we got so far?"

"Well, we have, books that somebody lost and somebody else found in a big hole, inside Ben Cruachan," said Eoin.

"Well now we're getting somewhere. Third line."

And far to the East, where the Gypsies are from

"Where are Gypsies, from?"

"Gypsies are all over the place."

An observation by Dan Campbell.

"I know, Dan, but where did they come from originally, where did they get their name?"

"It must be Egypt, surely, yes it's got to be Egypt," said Dan.

"Alright, sounds fair, let's go with Egypt."

Came a man with three ships and a dream and a song

"Right that's self explanatory, so what have we got now?"

"We have a man from Egypt with three ships full of books that he found, dreaming of bringing them and putting them in a big hole inside Ben Cruachan, whilst singing," said Eoin.

"OK, so far so good, next verse."

His hands and his face, they are scarred by a fire

"Alright he's been burnt."

Undeniable, wise man, never a liar

"Alright, intelligent and honest."

He holds all the truths that the ancients knew well
Be friends with this man, you are under his spell

"Well, what's all that about?"

"Hold on, hold on, Luath. Egypt, ancients, books, fire, spells, ships, dreams. I've got it, I think I've got it. We are looking for a wise man in a library."

"Don't be daft, Iain, there are no libraries in Alba, not yet, anyway. How did you work that one out?"

"Oh, but I think maybe there is one, and we're standing right on top of it, Dan, right on top of it, and the wise man we seek is inside. In ancient times the greatest library in the world was in a place called Alexandria."

"And where may I ask is Alexandria?"

"In Egypt, Eoin, in Egypt, that's where it is. And if you would all shut up, at least for a short time, I will tell you what I think.

All the knowledge in the ancient world was catalogued and stored in the famed library at Alexandria in Egypt, everything the ancients knew. And it was supposedly burnt to the ground and all the books and manuscripts lost. But our riddle tells us that a man saved three shiploads of books from this disaster, burning himself in the process and had the dream of taking them somewhere to re-establish them as a library."

"And how do you know all this, Iain?"

"Maybe because my brain works, unlike the rest of you cretins."

They were stung by the comment, but no one made a move. Iain's reputation was still intact.

"And why would somebody bring all these books to Alba?"

"Because they needed a haven, a safe place. I think our librarian is no angel and I think the Gods would be eternally grateful to our mysterious pirate."

"Why would that be?"

"These Gods are powerful, but power requires more power and for the Gods to have all the knowledge of the ancient world, allied to their own great forces, well I think they would accommodate the Devil himself."

"So we are looking for a librarian under our feet?"

"Absolutely."

"Let us see if we can locate him, what do you say? Next verse."

He will tell you the way and the path and the mean
He will tell you impossible, just but a dream
But if you hold a key that he wants and desires
He will show you the way to to content your own ires.

"All that means is he wants something for helping us, but we'll not know that till we get there."

The treasures he keeps they may win you a battle
But to speak to this man you must look to his cattle
They drink in the fresh and they bathe in the brine
And there's nothing in here that you'll say, is mine

"This is our trail, where's the nearest salt water to here?"

"Loch Awe is fresh, the closest salt is Loch Etive and the River Noe flows into the Etive on the north side of Cruachan. Down there, you can see it from here. The beasts will drink in the river and stand in the loch, salt water's good for their hooves and legs."

"The entrance must be on Etiveside."

The key to his door, it is hard to describe
It's not big, it's not little, but it is at low tide

"Entry is at low tide, so we might get our feet wet."

But inside it's so warm and so bright and much cleaner
Than the place that you left when life was much meaner
It's a room; it's a hall, an incredible court
Why not sit back, relax and enjoy a fine port

"What's port in this context, Luath?" Iain Campbell asked.

"Port, Iain, is an alcoholic drink that has not been created as yet, from Portugal on the Iberian Peninsula from a town called Oporto."

"And does the old meaning still apply as well, a place where ships come and go?"

"Absolutely, Iain."

"Well, Luath there are three ports on Loch Etive, Port Mor (The Big Port), Port Drobhrain (The Port of the Otters), and Port-na-Meana (The Port of the Mine), what do you think?"

"I think you're a genius, Iain Campbell, a genius."

"What did I tell you, Eoin, these Campbells are smart folk, I knew we could solve this little problem, just a little bit of application of the power of mind."

"Yes, Dan, I knew we could do it, in fact I think we had it almost solved before Iain stuck his nose in and gave us the answer that we sort of knew already."

"And what is the answer, Eoin?"

"Iain has the answer, Luath, he's told you already."

"Well, Eoin, you'd better take us there because we have little time left."

"Where are we going again, Iain, I kind of missed the end bit?"

"Port-na-Meana, brother, we are going to Port-na-Meana."

We came off the summit of Cruachan with a purpose, off the north side and dropped down into Coire Chat (The Corrie of the Cat) and

85

with Meall-nan-Each (The Hill of the Horse) on our left came into Glen Noe, our heading, due north till we reached the river, then we swung west following it's course, heading for Loch Etive. We made good time and we needed to. It was mid-afternoon of our second day and our time was precious indeed. We came closer to the mouth of the River Noe, then Eoin, who was at point shouted.

"There's your cattle, Iain, a fine heard of black Highlands, some in the river drinking and the rest in the loch just standing about enjoying the salt water on their legs. You're quite a man Iain Donald Campbell."

"Good, Eoin, we're on the right track then, take us left at the shore and Port-na-Meana is no more than a mile and a half from there."

There was pleasure and relief in the voice of Iain Campbell, but now it was down to the serious business of locating the entrance to this mysterious library.

"You haven't said much for a while, Tuppence, are you alright?"

"Yes, Luath, I'm fine. It's just that my mind is still on the top of Cruachan. I know I was there but it doesn't seem real somehow."

"Oh, it was real alright, but not real, like Strathyre, eh my little friend?"

"I'd forgotten all about Strathyre, Luath."

"Sometimes remembering is not the best thing to do, Tuppence."

BRENDAN

Our search began in earnest now but I knew fine that if there was an entrance here we would find it. Riddles were maybe not Dan's and Eoin's forte but their eyes missed nothing in country like this. We skirted the shore heading west. There was not a lot of time now for the tide was beginning to turn. We had maybe covered a mile when the rock formations ahead began to take on a far more interesting appearance. Tuppence could sense this and left my side and flew quickly to Eoin who was still heading our group.

"It's got to be close now, Eoin, hasn't it?"

"You don't take a lot of training, do you Tuppence, you can feel it too?"

"Yes, it's got to be close."

"I'll go round on the sea side of this next outcrop, Tuppence and you go over the top."

"Round here, Eoin, round here!"

"Well done! Tuppence, I think this is it. I'm going to take you stalking one day."

"I'd like that, that would be good fun."

The rest of us could see the activity ahead and took off after the two of them. As we came round the first outcrop of rocks we could see what the excitement was about. There was a second outcrop which formed a U shape some twelve feet high and about thirty feet deep, the U itself about ten feet wide, and at the back was a dark irregular shaped opening approximately five feet high and about three feet wide. We stood for a minute or so just gazing. Then the salt water made our next decision for us, the tide was now rushing in and with water lapping round our ankles, I said:

"Well lads, decision time, what's the verdict, last chance till next low tide?"

"Well," said Iain Campbell, "I can't swim so I'm going in."

"Did anybody think to bring a light?" asked Dan.

"No."

"Well in that case, let's get in there before we all drown."

We entered one by one with Eoin bringing up the rear. It was certainly dark and the tunnel seemed to go straight to start with. Gradually our eyes adjusted somewhat to the conditions. We could make out certain shapes and it was here that Tuppence proved very useful indeed. He flew ahead of us and the darkness didn't seem to affect him in the same way.

"I didn't know you could see in the dark, Tuppence."

"No, neither did I. It's not as good as daylight but I can see enough to guide you. I'll just fly ahead and see the lie of the land or the sea or whatever."

Tuppence was back in seconds.

"Well, boys the tunnel gets wider after about fifty yards and starts to gradually go uphill and it gets lighter the further along you go."

As we climbed there was no more evidence of seawater and as Tuppence had said there was a definite improvement in the light. The slope lasted maybe thirty yards then levelled out again and in a very short time we came to chamber, a room rough hewn out of the solid rock. Here there was a bluish, eerie kind of a light, but we could see clearly now.

The room was almost square and about ten yards across with a door at the far end, a heavy timber double door, studded and with elaborate hinges and handles. On either side of the door there was a stairway of stone. Had we arrived at the entrance to a library or the door to hell? There was tension in all of us except Tuppence who seemed to be perfectly at home.

"What do we do now?" said Dan.

"Knock on the door," Tuppence said in anticipation.

"Who's going to do that?" said Eoin.

"You do it, Eoin, you're the nearest."

"I'm not going to do it, you do it, you're the oldest."

"Iain can do it. He brought us here."

"This is all very fine but would one of you brave lads like to knock on the door?" I said.

"Why don't we draw straws?" suggested Eoin.

"Why don't the three of you all knock on the door together at the same time?" Tuppence suggested.

"What do you think, Dan?"

"Well, that would seem to be fair. But what do you think, Iain?"

"Pardon me for interrupting this little family discussion, but time is of the essence here. Would the three of you be so kind and walk up together and knock on that blasted door."

"If you put it like that, Luath, certainly."

"Thank you, it's much appreciated."

They approached the door rather cautiously and with broadswords raised they knocked simultaneously with the pommel end and promptly took a large pace to the rear, listening.

"There's nobody home, Luath, let's go."

"Give it time, lads. No one is going to reply that quickly, just hang on."

We all held our breath. Time stood still. I suggested that they try again, but once was enough for them. This is one of those times that you sort of lose purpose and meaning and you have no idea what to expect and you expect the worst and you hope for the best and you just wait, and wait. The tension almost had an odour, a smell of fear and aggression. There were three loose blades in the hands of men with a reputation, not for passive acceptance, but with willingness to strike first and pick up the pieces later.

Then it happened and how it happened! The door unlocked with a snap, both door handles turned at the same time with a creak and slowly the two halves of the door opened and it seemed to take forever and the sound of it trickled down our spines. Then through the blue light we saw a hooded figure silhouetted in the centre of the doorway for the light behind was far more intense than we had experienced in our tunnel. Then the voice – and what a voice! It was the texture of velvet, black velvet and it touched us together and we listened and we felt its warmth and its edge. It was a woman's voice, but not one of us had heard its like before. The words she spoke were these:

"We are expecting great company tonight, we will welcome the Hound of a King, the King of Little Birds and three Warriors of the Boar of Cruachan. If you are they, please enter, if not, you will perish where you stand."

"We will not perish for we are the ones you expect and our journey has been long and eventful."

"We are well aware of your journey, and you will be Luath, the Hound of Aedan Bhan."

"Yes, that is correct."

"And where's Tuppence?"

"Right here, beside me."

"In you come Tuppence, I've been looking forward to meeting you. We must talk later. Come and sit on my shoulder and I'll take you to the wise man you seek. The rest of you follow us."

"Well, Tuppence has certainly got of to a flying start," said Eoin.

"Thanks to Iain we're here and we are inside. Let's just take all this as it comes for we still have a mission and we cannot lose sight of that."

"We're all right behind you, Luath, you know that."

"Yes, I know that, but sometimes I wonder if you're not all better in front."

As we passed through the entrance, the doors closed behind us and it was only then we realised that we had other company; these other two had opened the doors for our hostess and were following close behind us, hooded also, with a few comments and some muted laughter. The language was a mystery to both myself and the

Campbells. But we could tell that they were also female. We were led at a brisk pace through what seemed like the main passageway. Every now and then smaller passages would cross the main artery and every few yards there was a doorway. It was all perfectly well lit and clean and the air was fresh.

In a very few minutes we entered a hall of similar dimensions to the one we first came upon, only this time there were several doors. We stopped and our hostess, still with Tuppence on her shoulder, knocked and entered the first door on the left. She announced our presence and we were invited in. The room was full to overflowing with books and papers and globes and maps and weapons and musical instruments. At a great wooden table sat a man half hidden by his treasures. He looked up and said:

"Good day and welcome to you all." He spoke in a great booming voice with an Irish lilt.

"Welcome to my library, I am Brendan, Brendan Mac-na-Mara."

"Thank you." I replied. "It is a pleasure to be in your company at last. May I introduce you to my companions."

"I think I know your companions, Luath, The Hound of Aedan Bhan, at least by name. It's good to see you Dan, Eoin and Iain Campbell and it's good to see you, my little King Tuppence. Are you quite comfortable on my daughter's shoulder?"

"Yes I am, thank you, Brendan. Your daughter is the fairest girl I've ever met."

Brendan laughed loudly and long, and said:

"Tuppence my little King, if Aphra is the fairest girl you've ever met, you have a serious eyesight problem."

"What do you mean Brendan?"

"Remove your hoods girls, let our visitors see your faces. Aphra is as black as the Earl of Hell's waistcoat, Tuppence. And my other daughters let me introduce you...this is Lu'an and she is golden with eyes the shape of almonds and this one is fair skinned but with red hair, and she is called Cara."

"I meant no offence, Brendan, I have never seen a black girl before and I've never seen one golden, but I have seen fair ones with red hair."

"There's no offence in your words, we all know our own colour; if we do not, then we live in a dream."

"Is this a dream, Brendan?"

"No dream here my friend, this is more real than reality."

Brendan Mac-na-Mara had shocked us already with his library and his beautiful daughters but he was to shock us again as he stood up. You could see that even seated at his table he was a big man and he bore the scars of a fire on his face and his hands and his hair was the colour of Cara's, and he did not look like a scholar. He had the appearance of a pirate. But then he stood and he was a giant of a man, closer to seven feet tall than six and I had seen him before and I remembered.

"You had two hounds once, did you not, Brendan?"

"I did indeed, Luath, and how would you be knowing that?"

"Because I met you once before in your own country."

"And where would that be, Luath?"

"At Cashel, Brendan, at the rock of Cashel."

"And why would you be at Cashel?"

"I was seeking the road to Cork, and I spoke to you and you had two Grey Hounds at your heel."

"And why was it that you spoke to me?"

"Because the man I had spoken to, not five minutes before, had sent me on the wrong road."

"And how did you know it was the wrong road?"

"Because the sun was in the wrong place."

"And did you wear the garments you wear today?"

"No, I wore the clothes of a different being."

"Did I give you the right road, Luath?"

"Indeed you did."

"Then my conscience is clear, and my honesty confirmed. But you have not come here to discuss the road to Cork, have you?"

"No, we have not, we have a mighty battle to fight against the invaders and we sought the assistance of the Gods and they led us to you."

"What do you want from me, how can I help?"

"We face serious odds in the battle to come, we must make our

Army three times stronger, but we have no reserves to speak of, we require inspiration and inspirational leadership. That is what we want from you."

"You realise what you ask are impossible dreams?"

"Yes, but we also know that it is within our power to dream, and a dream that is impossible is no harder to dream than one that is possible."

"Yes, that I understand, Luath. This library was once an impossible dream and yet it is here."

Brendan Mac-na-Mara folded his arms and turned his back on us for several minutes, deep in thought. Tuppence and I had witnessed a pose like this not three days before from another mighty man, but if the same thing happened this time at least Brendan's table stood a better chance of survival. But Brendan was different. He turned to us slowly, put his hands on the table and said:

"Yes I will help, but I make no guarantees. Success will still be in your hands. I am not a magician and I am no wizard."

"We all understand that, but we are all grateful to you Brendan Mac-na-Mara."

ᴄhe ᴄrᴀᴅe off  16

"There is one thing I require before I will help you."

"What would that be? If we have it you will have it."

"I have a problem in the Library that I have not yet found a solution to and we are falling behind in our work."

The others had all been very patient while Brendan and I conversed, but they all now saw the opportunity to be involved.

"What can we do to help?" inquired Dan.

"Yes," said Iain. "What is it that you require?"

"If we don't solve your problem, we can't move on. What is it?" said Eoin.

"Well, lads, the girls are aware of the situation, but none of us have come up with an answer yet. You see in this Library we have scholars and scribes and artists all working away restoring the books and manuscripts and maps that were damaged in the great fire in Alexandria. Some are smoke damaged, some fire damaged and some have been affected by water.

We brought all our equipment with us from the east and now some of it is beginning to get worn or broken or indeed lost, so we need replacements. The most serious situation is with the artists and you know what they're like. All their very fine pointed pens are useless so they cannot cope with the most delicate of detail. This is causing delays and incomplete work and we must push on. We have about forty thousand items requiring restoration."

"That's quite funny," said Tuppence.

"What do you mean funny?" roared Brendan.

"I didn't mean funny ha, ha. I meant funny peculiar."

"In what way?"

"Well you have forty thousand books to restore and we have forty thousand men to fight. It just seems a bit of a coincidence."

Brendan roared again, but this time with laughter and the whole company joined in.

"You're right my little friend, it is very peculiar indeed, and your forty thousand are as important to you as my forty thousand are to me."

"Can we see this detailed work that you need done, Brendan?" asked Eoin.

"Surely. There's an example on my desk, here."

The three brothers looked closely at the drawings on the manuscript, then looked at the girls, then looked at Brendan, then looked at each other and nodded.

"Yes we can solve your problem," said Dan. "But this is a job for an adult. I'll go."

"No you won't," said Eoin. "I'll go."

"Oh, no you don't, I'm going." said Iain.

"Please don't start this again, lads, we've been through all this before," I said.

"Why don't you draw straws?" suggested Brendan. "That would be fairer, wouldn't it?"

"Alright, straws it is. Shortest straw goes. All agreed?"

"Yes."

The girls prepared the straws and Lu'an held them out for the boys to choose. The Campbells chose their straws and held them up.

"Looks like you Eoin, but are you sure you know what you're doing?" said Dan.

"Absolutely! Is there another way out of here apart from through the water, Brendan?"

"Yes, several. Lu'an will show you."

"Now I'm slightly short of weaponry for this little task." Eoin said innocently.

We all sniggered, because Eoin carries more weapons about his person than the average small army.

"What do you need?" Brendan enquired.

"A short, light bow that pulls about fifty pounds and a quiver full of blunt arrows."

"You've no intention of killing anything then Eoin?"

"Not on this occasion. I'm aware of the company I keep, Brendan."

"Lu'an will show you the armoury, you will find what you need in there and she will accompany you on your journey."

"But, she's a girl."

"You're very astute Eoin Campbell. I know she's a girl, she is my daughter and she will go with you."

"I was merely thinking of her safety, Brendan."

"Look to you own safety, Eoin, believe me."

And with that, Eoin and Lu'an left our company for a time.

Brendan Mac-na-Mara proved a wonderful host and his daughters were splendid companions. We had an evening that will be remembered till this old mountain crumbles to the sea. He fed and watered us and gave us a remarkable tour of an incredible library. It was difficult to believe that we were inside a mountain. He showed us rooms where scholars studied and rooms where artists worked on ancient drawings, he showed us the places that scribes laboured and showed us old volumes being re-bound. We saw the armoury where men created weapons from ancient plans. This was indeed a treasure house. Then we came to another door and Tuppence said.

"What's in this room Brendan?"

"My little King, that is the one room that I cannot show you, I'm sorry."

"Why not?"

"Because if anyone ever finds out what goes on in that room the world will become a far more dangerous place than it is now."

"I see, I'll not ask again."

"But let me show you the Long Room."

"What's in there? There can't be much more to see, surely."

"Just you wait, my friends."

And, Brendan approached two mighty doors, three feet taller than the man himself and opened them and stood back and said:

"In there is my soul. Look."

We looked and we saw, and what we saw amazed us all, for none of us had seen anything to compare with this. We entered a cathedral of books. It was a great chamber eighty yards long, thirty yards wide with an arched ceiling some thirty feet high and it took the breath away. There was row, upon row, upon row of books and manuscripts and maps and drawings and incredible works of art and this old pirate looked at home.

"Can we read?" asked Iain.

"Yes, can we?" said Dan.

"If you Campbells can read, I have a strange kind of feeling that you're in the right place. Be my guest."

Brendan said that with pride and with pleasure as he turned two of Argyll's fiercest warriors into little boys in a sweetie shop. This was heaven to us all for all too brief a time.

Then the huge doors swung open again and there stood Eoin and Lu'an with no emotion on their faces and they marched forward in a determined manner. Brendan was standing behind the great table in the centre of the Library when they reached him. Eoin put his hand inside his plaid and brought out a little black cylinder about three inches long with brass at both ends and placed it carefully on the table in an upright position. There was silence and we all watched intently, for upon that little object our whole mission now rested.

"A gift from the Warriors of the Boar of Cruachan to the Son of the Sea, Brendan the Librarian," Eoin said in dramatic fashion.

"Will your gift perform as I asked?"

"You alone can tell, Brendan Mac-na-Mara."

Brendan slowly lifted the little cylinder from the table and carefully slid the two ends apart. He emptied the contents into a glass and we all saw, eight of the tiniest, finest and most delicate feathers you ever did see. They were like needle points, straight and strong and they tinkled when they hit the glass. Brendan looked up, walked over to Eoin Campbell and picked him up in a bear hug and swung him round and round laughing. When he finally put him down, Eoin said:

"I take it you like them then, Brendan."

"Like them! They are better points for the purpose than the ones we brought from the east. I am eternally grateful; Eoin, and I will never forget the service you have performed. But what bird carries such delicate feathers?"

"Only one bird carries feathers like these,
And you find her at twilight amongst open trees.
She visits in winter and stays till the fall,
And there is no reason why she leaves us at all.
She twists as she rises in her silent flight,
And in order to catch her, you must have rare sight.
The feathers I brought are the edge of her wings,
And a hunter like I am calls them her pins.
In the evening you'll see her, when you take a walk,
And her name? It is simple, she is the Woodcock."

"Well, you men surprise me, Warriors of the Boar. You also should be called Poets of the Boar and Scholars of the Boar. I have a library here with all the knowledge of the world and you bring me feathers that artists can use in the finest detail and my Library does not have this knowledge and you give me this knowledge in poetry. I have learned something this day, my friends. With all the knowledge in the world, I still have things to learn."

Tuppence spoke up. "We have delivered our due, Brendan Mac-na-Mara. Where do we gather the stones?"

"This will be your task, my little King. The stones lie to the west, over the ocean."

"Tell me where and tell me what they look like, and tell me how many for our time is precious and we have a battle to fight."

"Your silver thread from Danu will hold thirteen stones, one blue, four amber, three green, two white and one red."

"That is but eleven, there must be two more?"

"Yes, there are two more, you must find a pearl of black and a pearl of white."

"But where?"

"On the shores of Tir-nan-Og."

We all recoiled in disbelief. No one returns from Tir-nan-Og, for it is the land of the ever young, the land of the dead.

"Where is this place?" Tuppence persisted.

"It lies to the west, away to the west and no man has seen it, and no man has ever returned from its shores and no man has the courage to try."

"I am no man, Brendan Mac-na-Mara, I am a King and I fly and I will gather these stones. Tell me where and tell me when and this task will be done."

"Your heart is bigger than the Long Room, and if you achieve this, then you will have cheated death itself."

"If I cheat death on this occasion, maybe death will cheat me on another. I am prepared for this and it will be done."

"In that case, Tuppence, follow these instructions. There was a skirmish today at Dunstaffnage along the coast. Seven men died and in the morning Mananan MacLis will be there with his ferry to take the souls to Tir-nan-Og. His craft is white, it has no sails and it has no rudder and it flies across the ocean like a bird. If you can follow it and reach the shores of Tir-nan-Og, upon these shores you will find your stones and the stones you desire have little holes through them, put them on your silver thread and bring them back to Alba."

"This I will do, Brendan, with pleasure."

But our hearts all sank at that moment, for we knew it was impossible. My little friend had taken up the challenge and he would not get through tomorrow. And if he ever reached Tir-nan-Og how would he find these little stones on the shore? How many stones lie upon a shore?

We retired that night with nothing.

ICDPOSSIBLE

The next morning, the third day, we were up early, three Campbells, a hound and a fool. We stood in the outer chamber ready to leave and maybe we should have gone without a goodbye. But that was not possible; we held our ground and waited. Then Brendan entered and spoke.

"Your hearts are heavy this morning my friends, you think it's impossible the task that's ahead. Do not be discouraged. My faith is with you and the King you call Tuppence will lift your hearts before the night draws in."

"This we dearly hope, but hope sometimes, hope is clouded by reality, Brendan, and even the Warriors of the Boar sometimes harbour fears."

"You must go forward now, Luath, for there is no way back. The tide is low and the day will be long. But before you leave I have a gift for Aedan Bhan. You must see that he gets it. I give it to you Iain Campbell, keep this safe and be with the King when he opens it."

Brendan handed over a small silver baton to Iain. It was cylindrical and about six inches long. Iain took it and concealed it in the safest place possible, beside the hilt of his broadsword, and he said to

Brendan: "I promise you that this gift will be placed in the hand of Aedan Bhan, by my hand alone, no other hand shall touch it, no one will look in it, I will guard it with my life."

"You need not tell me that Iain Campbell for that is why I gave it to you."

"We had better be on our way," I said. "Goodbye Brendan Mac-na-Mara. I hope you have shown me the right road for a second time."

"One more thing before you go, my friends, I have another gift, but this one is for you. In fact there are three gifts. Three of my warriors will accompany you on your journey and they will stand by your shoulders till this matter is concluded. These gifts I give you are the most precious possessions I have."

And the door we had knocked on when we arrived opened slowly again, and we gasped in disbelief. For there stood three dazzling figures clothed in fabulous garments of war, with glorious helmets and chain mail and padded jerkins and sparkling accoutrements and lethal weaponry, just radiating martial power and fervour. It was unbelievable, the tallest in the middle wore blacks and greys and powder blues with a black burnished helmet intricately carved with a long spike on top and a slender nose guard with a cross piece and a neck collar and fringe of silver mail. The one on the left wore deep reds and scarlet with detailing in green with a helmet in burgundy carved dedicatedly, with a broad nose guard and wings and collar of black mail. The other was golden and shone like the sun, with details in red and yellow and a helmet with an eye mask and earflaps and vertical banding and a golden finial. These were indeed warriors to fight along side.

"I do not know what to say, Brendan, these gifts are beyond our worth."

"If that were the case, Luath, I would not offer."

"In that case, we will not refuse and we thank you, you have raised our sprits this morning. It will be a joy to fight alongside warriors such as these."

As the three warriors moved forward to join us, Eoin said:

"These Warriors are not what they seem, Luath, I know the

Golden Warrior on the right for it was she who brought the second woodcock to ground. I know the way she moves. That is Lu'an."

"You are indeed astute, Eoin Campbell. Yes you are right; the Warriors I give you are my daughters, Aphra, Lu'an and Cara."

"Then we cannot accept your gift, Brendan, the responsibility is too great."

"My daughters are responsible for themselves. Whatever happens to them is their affair. They have made their choice and they want to be with you and they have weapons that no man in this world has seen and they know the rules that govern yourselves."

"I was with Lu'an to hunt the woodcock, Luath, and if her sisters are remotely like her, then we have with us warriors that require respect. I think they should be our companions and if we fail, we will fail with dignity and beauty and I will not leave here without them."

"That, then is your answer, Brendan, we are indebted to you, but we must leave now or we will not catch our ferry."

We retraced our steps through the tunnels, seeking the light and the air of the outside world. But our joy was short lived because as we came out into the open air of Loch Etive we were confronted with a band of armed men. In a semi-circle round the mouth of the U-shaped rock outcrops stood at least thirty men with broadswords drawn and targes high. This looked serious and in the background were our old friends from Cruachan, Ammac-an-Geal and Ammac-an-Dubh, standing in the waters of Etive.

"Who are they?" I whispered to Dan.

"I'm not sure, but they look like 'broken men' to me."

"They don't look very broken to me, in fact they look completely whole," said Tuppence.

"Move to the front of the U and no further," said Aphra. "We can defend there and we can attack."

"Makes sense, Luath," said Iain. They will not come in at that point yet and we have choices."

"Let's do it then and quickly."

We formed ourselves at the mouth of the U, and we confronted an enemy that we knew nothing of until one of them spoke, and he spoke to Dan.

"I did not know it was yourself, Dan Campbell or your brothers, but we want the Hound and the Sparrow. If you hand them over you can walk free and there will be no blood spilt, and you can go home."

"I know that voice, from a long time ago. Ewan MacColl and the henchmen on your right and left are still the same, Archie and Dougie and why are the men of Rannoch here this morning? It couldn't possibly be for money could it now Ewan?"

"Dan, no harm will come to you, just give us the dog and the bird."

"This is not a bloody dog, this is Luath, the Hound of Aedan, and this is not a bloody bird, this is a King, you creeping, crawling bastard, MacColl." said Eoin.

The Campbell guard were like a coiled spring and I felt Iain Campbell preparing himself to slaughter with his hand poised over the hilt of his broadsword. This will surely end our mission, in sand slowly losing its salt water in an early morning. Then something happened that I had never seen before. I heard three little sounds, three little chinks of metal hitting metal and the daughters of Brendan all crouched and swung their right arms round their torsos to the left and they took a step forward with their right foot and their arms flashed and we saw discs, and three men died before they hit the sand, Ewan, Archie and Dougie, with metal stars deeply embedded in their skulls and our enemy took several steps to the rear and gasped. Their blades and their targes fell low, and they were stung.

"Do not stand in our way, you men of Rannoch, for we possess weapons and powers beyond your knowledge, but if you join us, you will share our power and our victory."

Dan Campbell has indeed a quick mind and he spoke again before the moment had passed. "Do you have in your company Ruiridh Mor MacDonald?"

"We have indeed, Black Dan Campbell, and he stands beside me, and I am his cousin Allan."

"Step forward, Ruiridh Mor," Dan said with the authority of a King.

Ruiridh stepped forward and spoke.

"I am the man you seek, but why?"

"You are the son of a chief, Ruiridh, you are a leader. You should not be on the moor. I knew your father and we were not always friends and did not always see eye to eye, but he was a fine man and he thought he had a fine son, and I think he has a fine son and you will lead this little army, and you will lead it beside me into battle and we will overcome any odds that fate decrees."

"I do not know if I am capable or worthy of this honour, Dan Campbell."

"Most of you men are without the protection of a clan or family and some of you might be considered rogues. This is no longer the case. You are now in the Army of Aedan Bhan and you men of the Moor now have a clan and it will be called the Rannoch Regiment and your Chief is Ruiridh Mor MacDonald."

There was a great cheer from these men, who not two minutes before would have gladly slit our throats.

"Choose your captains, Ruiridh, form your men and follow me and I will lead you to Hell and back, with my friends here of course."

"I will do this now with pleasure, Dan Campbell, but there is one thing, you ought to know."

"And what would that be?"

"There are another hundred of the Rannoch men lying in wait for your party, along the coast at Bonawe, just in case this little ploy failed."

"Well, you're the Chief now, make a decision."

"I'll send a couple of runners and inform them for whom they now fight, the Rannoch Regiment, and Ruiridh Mor."

"Good lad, now let's get moving."

"Well that was pretty close, Dan, do you think they are with us?" I enquired.

"They are with nobody else, unless you consider our friends from Cruachan, Luath, but let us be wary at Bonawe, for this thing has time to run yet, we are nowhere near our target."

We looked into the loch and we saw our 'friends' up to their calves in salt water, Ammac-an-Geal and Ammac-an-Dubh, still shouting, still swearing and still hitting each other with all the grotesque limbs they possessed. They will not like this twice, I thought.

"What's the opinion of our Alexandrian contingent?" I asked the close company.

"Just a fraction slow," ventured Eoin, and he ducked immediately as something star shaped and metallic whizzed over his head.

We had hard miles to go, but fortunately Bonawe proved a mere distraction and a hundred more joined our banner, although we had no banner. That was something to be remedied. We passed the Falls of Lora and Connel and headed for the old fortress at Dunstaffnage, and as we approached we saw what we all dreaded. The White Barge and Mananan MacLis taking on his cargo and we heard the sound of a dirge, three pipers playing 'The Lament for the Children', for the ones taken were mere boys, seven of them between the ages of thirteen and sixteen and you lose something at times like that, even though they are not of you. And you maybe gain something also, but what, I cannot tell.

"Tuppence, I called you a fool this morning, but you are no fool. I brought you here and I asked you to do this, but if you refuse, it will be accepted and things will be little different. It is not necessary my little friend."

"I was a little bird once, but now I'm a King and it was you that made me a King. Do you think I will not do this, when the whole world looks on?"

Tuppence prepared himself to fly with the barge.

"You know, my friend, this is impossible."

"Yes. I know it is impossible."

"Then go."

My friend took off to follow the barge, and the close company held their breath and prayed to whatever God would listen, and the sky grew dark in the east and she appeared again, Corvus Corone Cornix, circling the sky and she swooped down towards Tuppence and we could hear her voice, and she said:

"You are no longer the King of the Sparrows, Tuppence, you are now the King of all Little Birds, and I have brought your subjects to you and they will help you find the stones, you seek, and they will bring you home with your treasure."

And the sky grew dark, with a million little birds, flying west, with

Tuppence at their head and I was overwhelmed. The whole company could not believe what they saw, but we felt the air move with their wing beats and we heard the sound of a million voices. There were sparrows and warblers and finches and buntings, in fact every little bird you could imagine and some that no man had seen before. We watched as they disappeared over the western horizon and wondered.

ᴜᴀɪᴛɪɴɢ

In the hours that followed we tried to keep ourselves busy preparing for our return to the Aedan Bhan and the main army. Some local men joined our force, the three pipers volunteered and an old woman approached and said to us:

"I have been waiting."

"Waiting for what?" said Ian Campbell gently.

"Three warriors of the Boar of Cruachan, three warriors of the Pirate of Alexandria, a Great Hound of a King, a King of Little Birds and a Regiment of the Moor of Rannoch, and you made me wait a long time for this day."

"What do you mean, a long time?" Iain again said softly.

"I have a blue banner for you, made of silk and sewn with many colours and threads of silver and gold. You need a banner to fight beneath, you and your regiment?"

"Yes, indeed we do, but you are an old woman and you must have worked very quickly to complete such a task in so short a time. The Regiment was formed only this morning." I said.

"I worked very quickly to finish the banner, for I did not know when to expect you, I am in my ninetieth year and I am getting tired and weary."

The old woman produced a folded blue cloth from beneath her shawl and handed it to Brendan's daughters with these words:

"The Son of the Sea brought you to these shores, and he is very proud of his girls of colour, and he should be, because alongside Bheithir's magic waters, what you three do will be spoken of forever beside the evening fires of Alba. Now unfold your banner."

We all gathered round to watch this little ceremony. Aphra, Lu'an and Cara opened out this silken flag and laid it on the ground and its beauty was astounding. As the old woman had said, blue silk with many colours and silver and gold embroidery. It was eight feet long by five wide and again we gasped in admiration for upon the banner arranged with perfection were three wonderful boar heads, three mighty ships of the east, the head of a hound in the middle and above the hound's head was a little bird and on either side of the head were the letters R-R. I turned to the old woman and said:

"You did not create this masterpiece this morning."

"No," said the old woman. "I made it when I was a girl of thirteen. I told you I had been waiting a long time for this day to dawn."

"I'm not sure if I understand this. I'm not sure any of us understand this, but you are a remarkable woman and you have lifted our hearts while we wait for our friend. I just pray that we do not have to wait as you had to. But we do not know your name."

"I must go now," said the old woman. "My task is complete, but you must do something for me."

"Anything, just ask."

"When you reach Loch Awe you must immerse this banner in Bheithir's lost spring and if any of you suffer wounds in battle, you must cover the wound with this banner and it will help. And my name is Sine Bhan. When I was thirteen I was so fair but now I am ninety, you all can see."

And with that the old woman left and we were stronger, much stronger, but also weaker because we realised that we were selfish. Eoin went off to find a staff for the blue banner of the Rannoch Regiment, Dan and Iain went with Ruiridh to check the weapons and equipment and temperament of the boys from the Moor. Brendan's

daughters delighted everyone that they spoke to, and they played
with the children and talked to the old men of battles and spoke with
the women of hopes and fears and I kept a lonesome vigil awaiting
my little friend and thinking maybe it would be good to be
somewhere else just now.

We were losing the daylight and no sign and no sound and it was
not easy. No one came near me and I was pleased. I think they
understood. But the impending darkness made me uneasy. How
would they find their way back, if they knew the way back? But the
little bugger can see in the dark, can't he, I told myself. Yes of course
he can and there must be a million of them, they'll not get lost, will
they?

A few seconds later a hand touched my shoulder and I knew who
it was without turning. Iain Campbell said in a quiet voice:

"Luath, look, look to the sunset."

And I turned to face the west and the sun had disappeared behind
a black cloud.

"Yes, Iain, looks like rain again."

"That is not rain."

I turned again quickly and the whole company looked and our
hearts leapt. They were returning. The little birds had found the road
home, and they came closer and closer till we could hear their voices.
Then Aphra said in her voice of velvet.

"I pray our little King is still at the head, for they seem to be less
than when they left."

She was right. There were gaps in the ranks, but still there were
hundreds of thousands of them and they swept in like a storm. Then
a great roar from the Rannoch men on the sea's edge and bonnets
were thrown in the air and men danced with one another and then a
great shout:

"There he is, he's back, the Bird King is back."

And I sighed. There he was at the head of the largest army any of
us had seen and he swooped in and landed on Aphra's shoulder and
round his left leg was still the silver thread from Danu, but no stones.

"Tuppence, where are the stones, do you not have the stones?"

"No, I don't have the stones."

"You dozy stupid little bird. You mean to tell me you flew all the way to Tir-nan-Og and all the way back with me standing about here all day worrying, twiddling my thumbs and you stand there and tell me you don't have the stones. I just don't believe it! What the devil have you being doing and why do you not have the stones? The whole enterprise depends on the stones, you dope."

"I don't have the stones, Luath, my bodyguards do."

And Tuppence gave a little whistle and fourteen of the toughest little birds you ever saw swooped in and landed right in front of us, to the merriment of those gathered. There were certainly some mean looking characters in this lot, not to be crossed I thought.

"Just place your stones in a line in front of Luath, and I'll catch you boys later."

"You 'eard the King. Well get on wif it then. We don't have all bleedin' day!

"Place your stones!

"Wait fo-r it…! Wait fo-r it…!

"In a line. A straight bleedin' line, mind!

"Stand up straight!

"That flying f'ing on the left!

"Yes you! You horrible little tit!

"Yes you! The one wif that blue f'ing on your 'ead, and the filfy yellow tunic!

"I'll have you on a charge! Toute-suite! If you don't smarten your ideas up! Laddie!

"Place your stones! In a line! In front! Of the big dog! NOW!

"When I give the command. NOW!

"I mean, bleedin' NOW!

"Not next bleedin WEEK!

"Do you UNDERSTAND?

"DO…YOU… UNDERSTAND?"

"Yes, Yes, Sir."

"GOOD!"

And the wee birds placed their stones in a straight line right in front of me and flew off.

"See you later, Tupp, me old mate."

"Who's the one barking out the orders?" I asked.

"Oh, he's called Sarge."

"Sarge eh, well we could do with two or three like him in this outfit. What do you think, Eoin?"

"Absolutely, Luath, absolutely."

"Well what have we got here? One blue, four amber, three green, two white one red and one black pearl and one white one, all with little holes through them. Perfect, Tuppence, perfect. Tell me why didn't you put them on the silver thread as you found them?"

"We couldn't do it, none of us, it's not easy with beaks and claws, so I thought if we brought them back like this, the girls might do it for us, if they don't mind?"

"Of course we don't mind," said Cara. "We'll do it."

And the girls had them on the silver thread in seconds, and I looked at this little bracelet of stones and wondered how this little trinket would win us a battle. I looked into the eyes of Brendan's girls of colour and they answered my question, for they returned my look with a smile that soothed and reassured. There was something about these girls that was special. These were the girls in the dreams of Donald an't Sgian; these girls are perfection in mind and in body and in heart. I wondered if they were real and they smiled again and I accepted their answer with pleasure.

"Iain Campbell carries the Silver Baton for Aedan Bhan, we now need safe hands for the Stones of Tir-nan-Og. Who will carry out this duty?"

There was silence for a few moments, then I was aware of Eoin Campbell staring at me and I returned his stare.

"Are you thinking what I'm thinking, Eoin?"

"Yes, I think so, and I think you're right."

"Why do you think I'm right?"

"Because I thought of the same thing."

"Are you sure he's the right man for the job?"

"Without question, nobody better."

"Will you tell him or will I?"

"It's up to yourself, I don't mind."

"Alright, Eoin, you tell him."

"OK, I'll tell him."

"Tuppence."

"Yes, what is it?"

"Tuppence, would you like to summon Sarge, for me, and the rest of the Bodyguard?"

"Certainly, with pleasure."

There was laughter all round as Tuppence gave his customary whistle and Sarge and the Bodyguard came whizzing out of nowhere and landed right in the middle of our gathering.

"What is it, Tupp? What can we do for you?"

"Eoin Neil Campbell would like a word."

"I had better smarten me self up then, Tupp. Which one's 'e then?"

"The big one."

"There all big to me, Tupp, me old mate."

"Him over there, the one that looks like a mobile armoury."

Sarge flew over and presented himself to Eoin Campbell with the words:

"Sarge Montanus reporting for duty. SIR!"

"You don't need to shout, Sarge and forget the Sir bit, it's embarrassing."

"Alright, I understand, forget the Sir bit. YES SIR! Eoin."

"Right. The close company of the Rannoch Regiment, namely we in front of you just now..."

"Yes Sir I understand. You what is present at this particular moment, round about me, just now as I stand in front of you, here?"

"Mmm! Something like that. Yes. Luath, do you think we've made a mistake?"

"Nothing to do with me, Eoin, I never told you who I was thinking of for the job, now did I?"

"Thank you indeed."

"But he was my choice too, and still is, carry on."

"Right Sarge, we admired the way you found, brought and protected the stones from Tir-nan-Og and presented them to us safely and without damage here at Dunstaffnage, with your Bodyguard."

"Thank you very much indeed, Sir, Eoin, and may I take this operchancity to say what a privilege and pleasure it was for meself and me cohorts to assist in this great project what you have, ongoing here just now, at this particular time. What ever is ongoing, I'm not sure meself, but I'm sure somebody bleedin' knows. What the devil is going on anyway?"

"I'm not too sure meself, Sar...myself, Sarge, but I'm sure it will become clear later. What I'm trying to say is will you and The Bodyguard look after these bloody stones till we get to where we're going?"

"YES, SIR! EOIN! I mean yes, Eoin, consider it done, me old ma...Eoin."

"Thank you for bestowing this honour on Sarge Montanus and his King's Guard, Eoin. Very clearly and succinctly done with your familiar floral grammatical additions."

"It's a pleasure, Luath."

"Let's rest now for tomorrow we head back. Back to Aedan Bhan. Back to the army and back to the shadow of Cruachan."

the pass

There was some movement in the ranks to the rear, then the voice of Ruiridh Mor MacDonald bellowed:

"Stand fast, stand fast, the Rannoch Regiment. If one of you moves, you'll die by my hand, this glorious morning. This is now our challenge and we will take it up and we will not be found wanting. We are all with you, Luath, the Hound of Aedan Bhan, but you are now the Hound of Rannoch as well. Lead us forward and we will show you how we behave in front of our enemies."

"Luath."

"Yes, Iain Campbell, what is it?"

"You are not as you seem my friend, you are something quite different. The Hound of Aedan Bhan, the Hound of Rannoch, the Hound of Hell. You are no hound, Luath."

"Why do you say this?"

"You make men follow you. And men do not follow hounds, hounds follow men."

"You maybe think I am a shape shifter Iain Campbell?"

"Something like that."

"Do you follow me?"

"We all follow."

"Why?"

"I do not know, it makes me think deeply."

"Would you prefer to follow a mighty general?"

"I cannot say, but a mighty general you may well be, for we have not tasted battle yet, with you at our head."

"And when I ask you to lead this regiment's first charge into the enemy's centre, will you do it?"

"Without question, Luath."

"When I look at you Iain Donald Campbell, I thank the Gods that you stand with me and not against and if I am indeed what you suspect, you will be the first to see my true colours, this I promise."

"Maybe that would be something I would not want to see."

"Maybe, but we now have decisions to make. Would you call the others for me?"

The close company gathered again for we had to plan the route back to the shores of Loch Awe.

"Dan, I think we have two choices. Will you tell us what they are?"

"We have many choices. We could all commit suicide here and now. We could all disappear from here in every direction imaginable, we could hide inside ourselves and not come out or we could all just go away and not be remembered, but Luath gives us two choices. And why does Luath give us two choices? Because he controls us, this Hound tells us what to do, this Hound is manipulating us, this Hound is using us for his own glory. We have the right to decide for ourselves. I say we decide what our choices are."

"Dan, it is your choice, but you are here, like me, and I do this not for glory, not for myself but for us all."

"I will not follow, Luath, unless I see victory, and I cannot see it yet."

Then that velvet voice spoke, and Aphra's words were these:

"Dan Campbell you are a free man, otherwise you would not speak this way and what you say is true. We must make our choices and if you leave us now we will be weaker by far but our resolve will be stronger. Dan Campbell, do not leave us now for I have tasted slavery and you would not like it, a man like you. Another man came to me once and broke my bonds, a pirate with a red headed girl and took me from the fire and called me daughter. You know this man. And he took another and she stands beside me now and I have sisters and we are all different and we will never be the same, except we share freedom. This is why we follow the Hound of Rannoch and I think he also knows what a prison is like and his prison perhaps still holds him."

"Aphra So-Mali, you are the blackest girl I've ever seen with the purest heart there's ever been and I will gladly die beside you. We will meet the darkness together on the shores of Loch Awe. Now Dan, tell us our options for the return to the Army."

"Certainly, Luath, with pleasure."

"Thank you, and the next time you feel like ranting, would you like to do it out of earshot of the whole bloody regiment?"

"Sorry chaps, it won't happen again. Anyway we must return to Bonawe. It's there we choose our route, either north side or south side of the river."

"What's the best way?"

"The north side is easier but it's longer and we have to go through the Pass of Brander and round the head of the loch. I would guess from Bonawe it would be about fourteen or fifteen miles to Inistrynich. The route through the Pass poses problems though."

"What sort of problems?" said Tuppence.

"Well, the Pass of Brander is very steep and narrow. The path follows the shore of the loch and it's not wide. We could only go three or four men abreast for at least two miles, very susceptible to attack from above."

"Are we expecting to be attacked?" Tuppence again.

"We're not expecting it, but we must be ready for any situation that arises, we're not exactly going to a ceilidh at Inistrynich House are we now?"

"No, Luath. I don't suppose we are, but that would be nice, you girls would enjoy that, wouldn't you?"

"Yes, that would be wonderful, Tuppence," Cara said. "But look at us, we're not exactly dressed for a party now, are we?"

"I think you all look beautiful in your chain mail with all the colours and the shiny bits."

"Tuppence, excuse me for interrupting but we're kind of pressed for time. If you don't mind, can we discuss partying at some other juncture?"

"Certainly, Luath, carry on."

"So kind of you, your majesty. Right, Dan, the alternative?"

"South side, shorter, eight or nine miles, higher ground, more space, open country but we have to cross the loch. But there's a ferryman at Ardanaiseig, he'll take us across to Inistrynich."

"Sounds better, what's the close company's opinion?"

Nods of approval and agreement all round, but I still had reservations.

"Right we're agreed, but I think it's time to start using a few tricks, let us play to our strengths and our power is in our collective imagination. Let us now utilise our Aerial Reconnaissance Unit."

"Aerial Whatisance Unit? You're starting to talk all funny again Luath. Does anyone know what he's talking about?"

"Tuppence. Shut up and do something useful for a change."

"Like what?"

"Like whistle up The Aerial Reconnaissance Unit, you drip."

"I'm still lost, and you're still talking tripe."

"Whistle up Sarge Montanus and the Aerial Reconnaissance Unit, known to you as the Bodyguard, would you do that for me, Tuppence. Please?"

"I get it, you want Sarge and the Guards to go and have a wee look ahead for us."

"Yes, Tuppence, you've got it. That didn't take long now, did it? And what are you smiling about, Iain Campbell?"

"Nothing, nothing at all, I was just thinking about true colours, that's all, Luath, that's all."

Tuppence whistled and in they flew.

"What is it this time, Tupp me old mate?"

"You are now in charge of Aerial Reconnaissance as well, Sarge."

"Oh! That's fantastic, Aerial Reconnaissance; I've always wanted to be one of these people. What the bleedin' hell does that mean then?"

"Luath will explain."

"What's this stuff then, Luath, me old Do.... Sir?"

"You talk to me like that again, Montanus and your intestines will be stretched across a Welshman's long bow and you wouldn't like that now, would you? And he'll be singing at you."

"That is definitely serious, Sir, I make an unreserved apology, I was not aware of what I was saying at the particular time, what I was speaking to yourself, I have few faults but that happens to be one of them, talking meself into a spot of bo'ver."

"Your faults, Sarge, are our faults, but we don't say them, your loose tongue is refreshing and if we all spoke as you do, we might get along a lot better. But I have a little action for you and your cohorts and this is definitely serious."

"What would that be? Luath, me friend."

"I don't believe it," said Iain Campbell.

"What now?"

"Even the birds of the air follow."

"We need the birds, every one on this planet needs the wee birds, life without them would be dark indeed. Sarge, we have two possible routes back to Loch Aweside, one on the north side of the river and one on the south. I need to know if anything stands in our way, man, beast or Devil and I need to know before we reach Bonawe. Can you do this?"

"Luath, it's eight miles from here to Bonawe, you'll have this regiment there in two hours, won't you?"

"Without question, Sarge."

"Then we will meet you at Bonawe in two hours and I will have your intelligence report and do you know what, Luath?"

"What, Sarge Montanus?"

"This is why my mother made me and I'm bleedin' happy today."

"So am I, Montanus, and they will speak of you, wherever little birds gather and swear."

He left with his guards, and we left Dunstaffnage for Bonawe. We were there in just over an hour. These boys from Rannoch could keep pace and what pace! They glide over the roughest ground.

"Ruiridh, your lads impress me in movement but will they impress me in battle?"

"No one likes the boys from Rannoch but they all know one or two, and some are related in some way, and these boys will steal and they will kill sometimes but I will match this regiment with the finest in all Alba."

"We will see, Ruiridh Mor, we will see very shortly, before this day is done, I think."

We arrived at Bonawe with a little time to spare and we waited for Sarge Montanus and his squadron of heroes.

"Ruiridh, will you gather the close company to me and will you bring your cousin Allan and will you bring the pipers? I must have these boys from Carsaig and will you think for me Ruiridh Mor, for I have neglected this duty. Will you find me a man to carry our banner?"

"I will do all this, with pleasure.I will be back shortly... and Luath..."

"What, Ruiridh?"

"There are few days like this in a man's life and I'm glad I am here and not on the moor."

"Tomorrow, Ruiridh Mor MacDonald, Rannoch Moor may look like heaven to you and your boys."

Ruiridh returned shortly with all I had asked, the close company, the Ulva Pipers, Allan MacDonald and a boy I did not want to see.

"I have with me all you asked."

"Thank you. You boys from Ulva, how is your tutor? Is he still cantankerous?"

"He is, Luath."

"Does he still hit you on the fingers with his trusty feadan and does he make you run uphill playing?"

"Yes, but how do you know?"

"Because, I know him and I will know this day if he taught you well, and does he still drink whisky?"

"With relish, Luath."

"And what are your titles, my pipers from Ulva?"

"We have no titles. Sir."

"Do not call me Sir. I am the Hound of Rannoch and pipers that fight with me are titled because you are our passport to hell and we all go to war today. I need your names. Any name you give me will be recorded and if you fall, I will tell your mothers myself."

"We are brothers and our name is MacLean – Callum, Hector and Hamish."

"And do you know the tunes I require for this battle?"

"If we do not know the tunes then we have failed our tutor."

More brothers, I thought, our little story is full of brothers and brothers and sisters. But what will come now will shake my resolve.

"Luath, I have Allan with me, my cousin."

"Allan, you will be like Ruiridh, only better looking, big, strong and reliable and with a sharp mind and I'm grateful, and we'll speak when the others are in position and we will share some time, this I promise."

"I look forward to that."

"So do I, Allan."

"Luath, I have Angus with me, he should carry the standard."

"And why?"

"Because I think he's fit for the task."

"This boy is too young. If I put him on the field of battle, he will die this day."

"This boy has no intention of dying this day or any other day, Luath. This boy has in him something I have never seen before on the Moor of Rannoch."

"And what would that be?"

"This is difficult for me to say, and I mean no insult, but he is like yourself."

"This does not insult me Ruiridh, this just tells me why I am concerned with his safety. Will you permit me to speak to Angus, now?"

"Certainly."

"And will you be with me while we speak?"

"I will be with you, but is there fear in your heart?"

"There is always fear in my heart, Ruiridh and there always will be fear in your heart."

"Yes, but you are different. You are the leader in this and I am from the Moor, I live in fear."

"We all live in fear, Ruiridh, we are no different. But now I must speak with my fear. Will you bring Angus to me?"

Ruiridh brought with him a boy that radiated intellect and power and resolve and I almost broke seeing his face and I took a breath as deep as the ocean and I spoke.

"Angus, why are you on the Moor? You are too young to be there and too gentle."

"I may appear gentle, but I think you know that I am not. I've had fifteen years and little luck, that is why I live with the boys on the Moor."

"You're luck has not altered this day Angus, for what I ask of you, the mighty Hercules would think about once and decline."

"Hercules inspires many men, I inspire myself."

"Angus, you confirm my fears."

"Luath, you have no fears, you fear for others."

"I do not want this conversation, Angus."

"Nor do I."

"Will you carry the Banner into battle for your regiment from the Moor?"

"That is why I am here... and Luath...we share something."

"Do you think I do not know, Angus?"

"My great grandmother told me that one day I would stand by my father on a field of crimson and this time has arrived, has it not?"

"Angus, we will stand together on the field of battle and there will be blood and your friends from Rannoch will shed blood and the Campbell guard will shed blood and the bonny girls from Alexandria will shed blood and our little birds will shed blood, but I cannot tell you if we will be victorious for I cannot see further than you."

"But, what you do see, Luath is a vision."

"Yes, my boy. I have a vision, but my vision is mine and I do not know if anybody sees what I see."

"They follow Luath, don't they?"

"They would appear to, but do they follow a fool or a hero?"

"Luath, I know of three battles fought once and won."

"A long time ago, Angus, but things are different now."

"Are men different now, Luath?"

"Ruiridh Mor, do you listen still and do you understand?"

"I listen, but I confess I do not understand everything but I know you are not as you appear, Luath and I now understand why I chose Angus and I fear for the Rannoch Regiment and I wish I had ten regiments from Rannoch. We have bloody battles ahead and the great grandmother of Angus is Sine Bhan, is she not? And he will carry her banner and I am delighted to be here upon this day, but I know not why."

"Ruiridh, our quality and resolve is not in doubt, but our numbers still give me concern and I for one will gladly die in the company I keep this day."

"Luath, what are you?"

"Do not ask at this moment my friend, you will know me no better when you know me, and whatever I am, I will always be the Hound of Rannoch."

"Look, Luath, to the east, the birds return."

"Call the close company in Ruiridh, we all need to hear this report."

Sarge Montanus and his squadron swept down to us in close formation and landed.

"What does it look like ahead, Sarge?"

"Not very bleedin' good, Luath, both routes have armed men blocking the way east and they ain't flaming friendly."

"What's the situation north side of the river?"

"About seventy to eighty men high above the narrowest part of the pathway hidden amongst loose rock formations. If you went that way, they could drop half the bleedin' mountain on your 'eads."

"South side?"

"More men, over two hundred of the bleeders in between Ballimore, or what's left of it and Lochan an Cuaig and wif 'em is two of the most grotesquest creatures I have ever seen in my flamin' life."

"I see Sarge, you have done well. But what did these men look like?"

"Big ugly blighters and they are dressed differently than your Highland lads, they have some tartan, but they wear leggings tied up with straps of hide and padded jerkins and close fitting helmets and short swords."

"I think I know where they're from but you Campbell boys will know them better than me?"

"We know them fine, Luath," said Black Dan. Raiders from the north, raiders from Caithness and I suggest we take the southern road."

"Your suggestion is noted. And I suppose your brothers are like minded?"

"We are."

"Why do the men of Caithness raid here?" Tuppence asked the Campbell guard.

"Have you been to Caithness Tuppence?"

"No, never."

"Had you been, you would understand why they raid here. Argyll is the Garden of Eden and Caithness is the Wilderness."

"That will be the Campbell interpretation, Tuppence. Sarge if we took the northern road can we get above the eighty men in the rocks?"

"Yes, but not without the bleeders seeing you."

"We have a difficult choice."

"Luath."

"Yes, Sarge?"

"There is somethin' else I should tell you."

"Spit it out, Sarge."

"The two ugly creatures with the men on the south side have a dog with them."

"What about it, Sarge? Even the enemy are allowed dogs."

"This one is not there in freedom, this dog is chained and beaten."

"You think I should be concerned with every creature in this world that is mistreated. If that were the case I would become a social worker my little friend."

"Luath, listen to Sarge, he would say nothing if it were not important, he and his Bodyguard guided me through that terrible day at Tir-nan-Og, and I trust his judgement."

"So now, Tuppence, little birds tell me when to be concerned."

"Little birds can fly away, Luath," said that velvet voice from Africa.

"If a little bird told you, if I were you I would listen."

"Aphra, you can steady any ship, I will listen. Sarge forgive me for I look at the big picture and the details are sometimes overlooked. Tell me about this dog."

"Luath, you know this dog."

"I know very few dogs, Sarge Montanus."

"But, this dog looks almost like you, blue grey shaggy coat, fine features, long legs and a deep chest only slightly smaller and the chains cut its legs and its neck."

"This is no dog, Montanus, you fool, this is a hound, this is a deer hound, tell me more."

"I'm not from this bleedin' country, Luath, I don't know the difference between a deer flippin' hound and a deer flippin' dog, but I took my chance and flew down to speak to her."

"Her, you said her."

"Yes, Luath, her, are you bleedin' deaf?"

"I will ignore that, Montanus, but what did she say?"

"She said, do not tell Luath of my situation, tell him to go to the north side of the river and she said, he will find a way to overcome the men in the rocks, and her name is…"

"I know her name, Sarge Montanus and how did she look today, is she still bonny?"

"She is the most perfect creature from Heaven and she suffers terribly."

"Let us go south of the river and we will move with speed and we will destroy what is in our way and save what we all hold dear. Liberty."

Iain Donald Campbell spoke these words for me, for I had none, but I could see her face and I felt her touch and I was weak and they all knew this and they gave me their strength and I had never felt this way before and I must watch my tongue when I get through this.

We moved in silence for two miles or so then a hand touched my neck and a gentle voice from the east said softly.

"Her name, Luath, what is her name, this creature from Heaven."

"Her name is Laggan."

"She means a great deal to you, Luath, our leader."

"Lu'an, you call me leader but at this moment I lead no one, not even myself. It is you who lead me."

"No, Luath, we only hold you close just now, till you are ready again."

"I have companions I do not deserve, Lu'an."

"No, Luath, you have no companions here, we are your family, you are our father, we look to you for guidance."

"And when victory becomes defeat, what then?"

"Look around you, Luath? What have you here? These three Campbells they are all leaders themselves and they follow you. Why? The boys from Rannoch, they follow. Why? The pipers from Ulva, they follow. Why? The birds of the air, they follow. Why? The daughters of Brendan, we follow. Why?"

"Lu'an, I see it, your lesson is over and you say things I want to hear. Would you be so kind as to bring the close company to me, for I have a plan."

And this bonny girl from the east leaned over and kissed my ear and it is a long time since a woman kissed my ear, too long. The close company gathered.

BALLIMORE

"Over two hundred you said Montanus, between Ballimore and Lochan-an-Cuaig."

"Yes, SIR."

"Ruiridh, how many men do you have?"

"We lost three on Etive side, our number is now one hundred and twenty seven."

"Right. This is what we do, we divide our force in three."

"Why would we do that?"

"In order to win, Eoin, that's why. Are there any more objections? Tell me now for this is the strategy and the rest I will leave in the hands of the captains.

Ruiridh Mor MacDonald take thirty men and head for Shellachan then take your men between Dubh Loch and Loch Tromlee and come in behind the settlement of Ballimore and conceal yourselves there, till you get the signal.

Allan MacDonald take thirty men and head along Creag-an-Aoineidh and on the north side of Lochan-an-Cuaig you will find a cave, hide there till you get the signal and do not be seen from the north shore of the River Awe."

"And what will the signal be?"

"The pipers will play three tunes. The first will be an insult to the enemy, the second the charge and when the third begins you will join us from the flanks, but also a little bird will tell you when. Pick your men Ruiridh and Allan, leave us now and join us under the blue banner and the blood of Caithness will be spilt today, and you two MacDonalds, I know this will not sit well with you, but your war cry today if you will accommodate me, will be Cruachan. I want these men of Caithness to believe that every mother's son from the whole of Clan Campbell is upon them; you will understand when you hear the third tune."

"Shouting the Campbell war cry will not harm us for one day, Luath, but we will do this only once."

And with that, sixty men left us, and took a little part of me.

"You leave us seventy six warriors, Luath, to attack over two hundred."

"Yes, and what of it Dan Campbell? Maybe you should consult your shop steward and check it out with the union. If you do not wish to be here, we will have seventy five. Do the girls from Alexandria object also?"

"We accept the challenge, there is no glory in defeating an inferior force," said Cara.

We could see the enemy now in the distance formed in a line across our path, standing three deep, their front would be almost one hundred yards wide. I addressed our seventy six.

"Listen closely, for what I say now, you must do. The enemy must be persuaded to keep its present formation so we will form as they do and mimic them in a line one hundred yards across but our line will be single and we approach them in this manner.

On the command "Form Up" we change our shape and condense into an arrowhead formation open at the rear and charge their centre. This manoeuvre will be done at speed. The close company will form the point of our arrowhead and the boys of Rannoch its cutting edges. The standard bearer, the pipers, the King's guard, myself and Tuppence will be in the little pocket just behind the point and I will command from there. Do I make myself understood?"

All seventy-six replied in the affirmative.

"Good, but I have a request."

But Iain Campbell was already aware and this rock of a man was smiling and my admiration for him soared again.

"Yes, Luath without question."

"In that case the Regiment of Rannoch, form your line on either side of Iain Donald Campbell now. Angus, unfurl the Blue Banner. Callum MacLean, your action will be the first and which particular insult will you and your brothers hurl at these men from Caithness?"

"We will play 'The Carls wi' The Breeks'."

"You know your history, Callum, like your tutor. In that case, Pipers strike up and let us move forward."

We moved forward at a measured pace towards the enemy, our thin line looking fragile to the eyes of Caithness. I prayed also that Ruiridh and Allan would be in position by now. This is the time you feel frightened for your charges, this is the time The Gods make you suffer, this is the time to be in another world. We came closer and closer and closer and I could feel he Regiment of Rannoch in tension and Caithness understood our insult and reacted with jeers and shouts and their line wavered and almost charged. We had their sole attention now; we were their target. The time was upon us.

"Montanus send your friends to our flankers and Callum sound the charge, 'The Standard on the Braes of Mar', and Rannoch, Form Up!"

And they formed up with incredible speed and charged and they leapt forward with a certain Campbell at their head and they kept their shape and drove into the centre of the foe with a fury that was devastating and the Caithness line buckled and was wrapped round our arrowhead in seconds. Highland blades whistled and heads danced and gruesome magic from the East was performed and limbs fell to the ground still twitching and I shouted to MacLean:

"Your third tune, Callum, what is it?"

"'The Campbell's are Coming'."

"Strike up my boys from Ulva, bring the Campbells in from the flanks."

And inside the count of three the cry could be heard above all other sounds. "CRUACHAN, CRUACHAN, CRUACHAN!" and Caithness heads turned to the north and turned to the south and thirty men from the north and thirty men from the south coloured this lonely green field red with fluted blue blades from Ferrara and not one man from Caithness walked away and little girls and little boys in the far north will weep this night for their fathers are not there any more and I do not like this part.

"Ruiridh Mor, find Laggan and release her, bring her to me and Allan MacDonald, I require a casualty report immediately and Tuppence, Sarge and the Guard sweep this ground for me. I need to know if anything else lurks here for we will be with Aedan Bhan this day and Ruiridh Mor MacDonald, your boys from Rannoch cover ground with speed and ease and they fight with passion and panache and I have not had such a day as this for a long, long time and the close company, you took the brunt of the onslaught, how do you fair now?"

Eoin Campbell spoke for them and said:

"Luath, you are the complete bastard. Why men fight for you I do not know, you sent us to Hell today, seventy-six against over two hundred and we all carry wounds. Iain my brother carries the most, and I do not know if he will survive this, and our girls from Alexandria bleed and we all bleed for you. Why? I do not know. But I tell you this, my friend, no one can take this hour from me and I would not swap it for all the hours I've had before or all the hours there are to come."

"Eoin Campbell, I regret nothing, but I would not have sent you in if you could not do it, for my faith is you and the company you keep."

"Iain needs assistance quickly. We do not want to lose him. He was at the point and he shielded us from the fury."

"And who shielded Caithness from Iain Campbell's fury? No one. You all saw the Devil today and tomorrow, Eoin, things will be more difficult. I will do all in my power to aid your brother and if it is any consolation I consider Iain my brother as well."

"Luath, our casualties are few," said Allan.

"What are the figures?"

"Seventeen dead and twenty-three wounded."

"I do not consider that few. The more we lose today the less we have tomorrow."

"But, Luath, Caithness was devastated today, not one of them walked from this field."

"Caithness is Caithness, Allan MacDonald but we are Rannoch. Every drop of blood we have is precious, our wealth is in the boys with a broadsword in hand and a smile on their faces. We must treat them like gold dust. Do you understand me Allan?"

"I think I do."

"Good, my friend, now bury our lads with dignity and a piper playing and tend the wounded and leave Caithness for the vixen."

Then a voice said: "You change little, Luath and I do not know why I care for you, for you are a brute and these here will know this by now and yet they are still by your side, as I am."

"Laggan! It's good to see you. How are your wounds?"

"Deep, Luath."

"I see, no forgiveness yet. I understand, but will you be with us tomorrow? I need you close."

"I will be close, but I will take no part."

"As long as I see you, I will be content."

Then Lu'an came and spoke to Laggan and they left me together and I silently thanked Brendan for his daughters again. Tuppence and the Guard returned.

"What is your report, Tuppence?"

"There is evidence of another force near this field today, Luath, to the rear of the Caithness position, about a thousand yards behind but they are not there now."

"How do you know?"

"There is an area of heather that is flattened and it looks like men have concealed themselves there for quite some time."

"But they're not there now you say?"

"No, Luath, there is no trace of them now."

"What do you think, Dan Campbell?"

"I think exactly what you think – Donald and The Eyes of the Army."

"So we were not alone today, and Aedan Bhan will know we return on the evening of the fourth day and what story will Donald tell, Dan?"

"Donald will not be short of words if he saw us today."

"So, do you think we might return with a bit of a reputation?"

"That may well be the case."

"Good. Tuppence did you see our friends from Cruachan, the brothers Black and White?"

"I did."

"And what were they doing?"

"Fighting, as they did before on Cruachan and on Etiveside."

"They will not like us, I fear."

"No, Luath, but they are lost now are they not?"

"They are indeed lost, my friend but they will be with us always, for they are our conscience and every time you look round they will be there and when you choose you will pick one and defy the other. They will not go away. I'm pleased that they still live.

Tuppence, call all our friends together for our quest is over and now we must fight for a country that some of us hate and some of us love, but we all know it is as cruel as we are and we are cruel indeed."

They gathered by Ballimore. I looked at them and they looked at me and our peace was made there and I spoke to them.

"We have an almighty battle ahead. You bled today with me, but this was but a skirmish. Tomorrow will be different. You will all suffer and you will lose friends and the day might reveal our weaknesses, but it will also show our strengths and if any of you want to leave, do so now, I will take no man or woman into conflict, that does not desire to be there."

"What about bleedin' birds Luath?"

"Sarge Montanus you little bastard, if you leave with your cohorts, tomorrow is lost."

"We will not leave your side, never, for no one treats little birds the way you do, we have status in your army and we carry the stones from Tir-nan-Og and I can't flamin' figure out what the bleedin' stones are all about, but I have to know."

"Tuppence, you have the finest guard any King has ever had, but do you know this?"

"I know it and when I think of Tir-nan-Og, I shake with fear."

"We must move forward to Ardanaiseig to the ferry, we must be with Aedan Bhan tonight."

Then Aphra said:

"Iain Campbell is failing fast, Luath."

"Aphra, what did Sine Bhan say?"

"She told us to immerse the Banner in Bheithir's lost spring and it would help our wounded."

"Then we must do so. But where is the Lost Spring?"

"None here knows."

"Then we must find out and quickly."

ᚈᚻᛖ ᚈᛖᚳᛈᛖᛋᛏ

Ardanaiseig was close and when we came off the high ground we saw the head of Loch Awe with its islands and crannogs and its beauty and in the distance on the east shore we saw an army in preparation. We found the ferryman with no trouble. His name was Alasdair.

"Welcome, Luath. I have been waiting for you and your mighty army."

"And how did you know we were approaching Ardanaiseig?"

"A young dark haired boy with two hundred Campbell broadswords told me not three hours hence."

"And his name would be Donald no doubt."

"His name was Donald and he told me to ferry you and your friends safely to Inistrynich for you are needed to colour the shores of Loch Awe."

"How many birlinns do you have?"

"Enough for this task for you are the smallest army I have ever seen."

"We are indeed small for an army but you will carry more men than you think on this crossing, Alasdair."

We filled Alasdair's birlinns and left the west shore and headed for the middle of the loch then Eoin and Dan spoke to me again.

"Luath, our brother Iain is dying. His wounds are horrific. He should not even be here now."

"Before we go further, we will find Bheithir's lost spring. The ferryman might know. Alasdair, have you heard of Bheithir?"

"Yes, but why ask such a question when you go to war?"

"I need to know where the Lost Spring is and quickly."

"Bheithir's Lost Spring? You tease me?"

"I tease no one, Alasdair, I need to know now."

"Luath, we are sailing on the Lost Spring, the Lost Spring is Loch Awe, do you not know the story?"

"No, I don't know the bloody story. Angus, quickly unfurl The Blue Banner and immerse it in the loch and cover Iain Campbell with it. Now."

Angus did as he was told, and Iain Campbell was covered in the banner and he was saturated with the waters of Loch Awe and his eyes closed and he slept and we watched and we prayed and Brendan's girls never left his side and we all prayed again.

Then certain things started to occur that no one on board could have foreseen. I knew something would happen because this is the most potent acreage in the whole of the Gaidhealtachd, where the seeds were sown all these years ago.

Alasdair had five birlinns plying the loch carrying people and goods and cattle and now armies back and forth, but he did not account for the Regiment of Rannoch. The weather was fair as it had been for several days since we started our journey but as we passed by Innishail our lives were changed forever.

A wind began to blow and it came from nowhere and the boats began to heave and the movement was violent and a great noise filled our ears and it was a sound from another place and I prayed that Rannoch would hold firm but fear was in their eyes and the waters began to boil and the smell of sulphur was in the air and a high pitched whine made all of us deaf and a flash of light made all of us blind and then it started raining and it stung our faces and burnt our skin like molten metal from above. But Rannoch held its faith.

Then silence, the waters calmed, the wind died, a mist surrounded us, the smell was gone, and Iain Campbell was standing in the centre of the birlinn, tall and strong with only scars where the wounds had been with Sine Bhan's banner in his left hand and Ferrara's broadsword in his right.

Then we saw an army emerging out of the mist towards us on Loch Awe and they walked upon the waters and Rannoch was tense and I was devastated. Why do they make me suffer more? Then I saw faces from times that I had left, and I saw the dark tartans of green and black and gold that I once wore and saffron robes that clothed me too and fear gripped me. At the head of one thousand was the only man I feared and the only man I loved and his image is engraved upon my soul. He was tall and straight and elegant and he had the face that made men jealous and the face that made women weak and he did not smile, but he smiled a lot when I was a boy and he laughed. And I knew this man well and he was the warrior that warriors fear and he was dark as always and dressed for war and in his right hand, loosely held, was the sword made in Vulcan's forge, four and one half feet it's blade, burnished with the soot of Vulcan's fire with a hilt for two hands and balanced by the Gods of War.

The enemy trembled in fear when they heard it whistle and sing and I have seen men split in two from skull through pelvis with one stroke of this terrible blade and he went into battle bare headed and free and he did not know the fear of death and I became strong again. He spoke to Iain Campbell and said:

"Someone has sent you to a Hell today that no man should see. You were the point of the arrow, and you won. But do you trust this man that you follow? I know him, for he is of my blood. Know that no man expects more from his men, nor expects less than the hand you give him. Three times I have faced the foe that you face tomorrow, with that same leader, and we won every time, but at a terrible price. If you do choose to fight tomorrow, if you are content with what lies ahead, know that I will be by your side. And although I am dead, I will cloak you in armour and your name will be written in the blood of the slain.

We leave you now, for our battles are over, but I will see you in time. They called me the Black Prince. And the one who leads you in your mighty quest is the only one alive you can trust."

Iain Campbell turned to me with that terrible black blade in his hand and found my eyes and said:

"I know you now in your true colours. You are Am Mhathan and I thought so, and I prayed so. I know now why we follow and tomorrow will not come soon enough for me."

And he collapsed on the deck and slept. Aphra turned to the ferryman and spoke to a man shaking in fear and said:

"Who lies on Innishail Alasdair?"

"The descendants of Uther sleep there but I did not know that they still moved amongst us and I am filled with fear, for there is nothing more ancient or terrible than they, unless the hills, Am Mhathan and the Devil."

I said:

"Inistrynich beckons. Let us move forward for we have plans for tomorrow and we must be with Aedan Bhan tonight. He will be seeking our company now and we will not let him down."

And they looked at me and they did not understand, but they accepted and they all looked tired and I felt for them because they give me the power to go forward and not to look back and if we emerge on the other side of tomorrow intact it will be a miracle.

ᴄʜᴇ ɴɪɢʜᴄ ʙᴇꜰᴏʀᴇ

As our birlinns approached the landing point at Inistrynich we could see the preparations in full swing. This was indeed an Army ready to fight, with some contingents drilling while others checked and sharpened weapons and the young lads with the garrons distributed rations and men fed themselves. We could hear their voices now; Gaelic mingled with Welsh and the tongues of Scandinavia with the raised voices of the captains barking out orders. It would appear that Aedan Bhan had not only held this army together but united it as one and it was a delight to see them in this state of readiness.

Slowly our birlinns drifted in as the oars were raised from the still waters and heads turned towards us and men fell silent and all activity ceased and the silence was deafening. We tied up and disembarked and how that army saw us then was of great importance.

"RANNOCH, FORM UP! IN COLUMN."

And Rannoch formed up in column with great speed and precision three abreast with our pipers at the head, with Angus the Bannerman and myself, followed by the Alexandrians and the Campbell Guard, and with Ruiridh and Allan MacDonald heading the main body from the Moor. Tuppence and the King's Guard flew above the head of the column.

"Angus unfurl the Blue Banner."

"Callum MacLean, your tune is 'The March to the Battlefield'."

"Sarge Montanus, lead us to Aedan Bhan, the Ard Righ."

"RANNOCH! FORWARD."

And the pipers played and we moved forward towards the army we left a few days before and our reputation preceded us for the army parted and allowed us unhindered passage to the tent of Aedan Bhan and as we passed them a great cheer echoed along the shore from the throats of thirteen thousand and Rannoch joined this army with pride and dignity.

Sarge Montanus led us to Aedan's tent unerringly and the regiment halted outside and the close company sought entry and we were invited inside. Aedan Bhan, Donald an't Sgian and The Druid of Carnac confronted us with the leaders of the Welsh, the Irish and the Scandinavians at their rear and we stood there and waited for our invitation to speak and I did not like that and it was in my mind to send them all to Hell that night, but that would not have been desirable at that moment and I softened myself again.

"Luath, I sent you on a mission with a King to bring me an army to defeat the Men of the White Dragon. What do you bring here this evening?"

"I have with me what is necessary."

"And pray tell me what that might be."

"Stand forward Iain Campbell and come forward Sarge Montanus and give Aedan Bhan his army and his strategy for tomorrow."

And Iain Campbell stepped forward and handed Aedan the Silver Baton that he kept by the hilt of his broadsword and Montanus gave Aedan the stones from Tir-nan-Og and retired with grace.

Aedan Bhan opened the silver baton which revealed a poem from Brendan and he looked long and hard at the bracelet of stones and he said with the venom of the viper:

"I sent you on a mighty mission and you return with one hundred rogues from Rannoch, three Campbells, three women, one black, one yellow and one red, two MacDonalds, three pipers from Ulva, a blue banner, a squadron of little birds, a poem and a bracelet of coloured stones. You have failed in a mighty way, Luath and you will die tonight before you disgrace this army more."

"Aedan Bhan, there are only eight men that have the opportunity to die tonight and you stand in front of us now."

Iain Campbell had that terrible black blade bared already and his brothers followed, Alexandria followed suit and so did the MacDonalds.

"This will not end in bloodshed," Donald an't Sgian said with the authority of a King.

"Aedan, why would they return if they brought nothing? Listen to our friends for I saw them today at Ballimore and they behaved as we dream and I hope our army will behave tomorrow as they did today. And Allan and Ruiridh Mor MacDonald how did this terrible hound persuade you to cry "Cruachan" when you attacked Caithness?"

"He merely asked, as a gentlemen does," Ruiridh replied.

"That is good enough for me, Ruiridh Mor MacDonald, and if you will you permit me, may I attach the Eyes of the Army, Campbells every one, to the Regiment of Rannoch for tomorrow for we will not be needed anywhere else?"

"You are most welcome, my friend, and maybe we can teach you Campbell boys the finer arts of warfare."

"Maybe you will teach, Ruiridh, but I also think you will learn."

"Donald Campbell, enough! I am still Ard Righ and I will listen. Tell me what you have brought for us, Luath."

"Read the poem from Brendan with Iain Campbell and permit our girls from Alexandria to speak with the Druid of Carnac about the stones from Tir-nan-Og."

"This will be done now. Let us read this poem together Iain Campbell, and your girls can go with the Druid, for these strange things I do not understand."

And the three most enchanting girls of colour and war left with the Druid of Carnac and I knew that he would learn things that night that he could never have dreamed.

And Iain Campbell read Brendan's poem for Aedan.

AEDAN'S POEM

If we walk this world, who is to blame,
You and I, are we both insane.
You are a King and I tend the Books,
Do we do this for fun, or is it just for looks?
But I say this my brother, do not take this fight,
You are faced with poor odds and incredible might.
The men that you face are both callous and mean,
And the likes of them here, should never be seen.
But there is a time and it comes to us all,
When we must stand or we will surely fall.
And if this time is near and I feel that it's come.
It's clearly the time that things must be done.
But I am not you and you are not me,
The decision you make, is from what you can see.
And my power is with you, if I can assist,
And we'll blow them away, like the will o'the wisp.
But if the day is upon you, and you must fight,
Let the man from Carthage be your might.
He defeated Rome, with a line and a circle,
And an Emperor fell, in his garments of purple.
I'm a pirate, a bookman, a scribe and a scholar,
You must convince the enemy, you are much smaller.
You must show him you're dull and simple and heathen,
Give him nothing at all, no rhyme and no reason.
Then you form a line that is low and degrading,
Give him the high ground; don't show him your shading.
He'll advance at your centre, with all of his might,
Give way, form your circle and squeeze it so tight.
And if you perform this, as well as you can,
They'll be singing your praises, the Great Aedan Bhan.
And the darkness will lift from off of your heather,
But the shore land will just get redder and redder.

"And what kind of man writes poetry like this for Aedan Bhan, Iain Campbell, and do you know what it means?"

"A giant of a man from Erinn wrote this poem for you and he is a Librarian and he also gave you his most treasured possessions, three daughters, one black, one yellow and one red, and if you do not accept his gifts, by the morning no Campbell will fight alongside you and if you do not understand this poem, do not fight tomorrow for you will not be triumphant."

"In the poem, I hear a brother speak to me but I do not know who the man from Carthage is and that is the key, is it not?"

"That is the key. And in Brendan's library I read about this man. Hannibal was his name and he fought a campaign that lasted twenty two years and he defeated the finest Army in the World at Cannae with a line and a circle and tomorrow you will do the same, if you have the courage."

For hours Iain Campbell and Aedan Bhan analysed that mighty battle fought in the mists of time and they slowly became friends and our Alexandrians worked their magic on the Druid of Carnac. Then Tuppence said: "What are we doing tomorrow, Luath?"

"Not a lot, Tuppence, but before you sleep my little friend, come with me and be amazed, for tomorrow is a long way from here and a shortcut to Hell."

And we moved amongst this army that rested for a night of torture, a night of regret, a night of fear and a night of hope, and we saw the faces of men from all over our precious world and we knew that some if not all of these men would be silent and cold by this time tomorrow.

We spoke to men from Uppsala and Stavanger and Trondheim and Odense and they smiled and laughed at death and treated us with respect and these men from the north had our respect for they would fight with us on our soil, in our war, but also it was for them.

And we followed the low deep voices as they sang, men from Cader Idris to Caerphilly and these men possessed weapons that shower the battlefield with death from the sky and there were not many, but maybe we did not require many and they laughed with us as we passed and they always sang.

Then we moved amongst Erin's contingent, boys from Strabane and Fermoy and Tralee and Kilkenny and you would have thought that they might be going to party and maybe they were for they showed no fear of what lay ahead and maybe that moment was enough and these men would die having laughed.

We then passed the Highlanders before we retired, MacLeods from Harris, MacDonalds from Sleat, Camerons from Loch Eil and Campbells from Breadalbane and many, many more and I prayed they would save their own battles till after tomorrow, for these men also see what is in front of them and they react, but this night the feuds just simmered.

"Tuppence, did you see their faces? All I say is remember the men you saw tonight for the ones that die give the rest of us life."

"Luath, I am really scared."

"I am really scared as well, my little friend, but this will not stop our progress. Now is the time to rest and I will be with you in the morning early. Good night."

"Luath?"

"Good night, Tuppence."

I left my friend to himself that night and I did not enjoy that, but everything was in place for tomorrow. But I had one more task to perform and I found the man I wanted to speak to.

"Iain Campbell, you have directed Aedan Bhan?"

"I have, Luath, with the knowledge I possess."

"Good, for I have something to tell you."

"You need tell me nothing, Am Mhathan."

"But I must for our friendship has left you scarred for life."

"Every scar I have is precious to me, for I gained them with you on the field of battle and no one can take them from me."

"Iain Campbell, you know me now and I tell you this, that I am permitted for one solitary day in every year that passes, to be myself and the day I choose is tomorrow and I will be at your shoulder as we charge."

"So tomorrow I will charge with Am Mhathan?"

"Yes."

"Then sleep will not be my friend tonight and tomorrow can last one thousand years for all my cares and will the Black Prince's armour protect you also?"

"No, that is for you alone, I have no protection and I deserve none."

"Why?"

"Because I killed once when I should not have and the one I killed was the finest hound that ever chased a stag and his name was Luath, and Laggan despises me still."

"So you live his life now instead of yours?"

"That is my penalty and I dearly regret my actions, but tomorrow Iain Campbell you go into battle, with a companion that has the speed of the hound and the power of the bear."

"I fight with the hound and the bear beside me tomorrow, then I have all I require and I ask for nothing more."

"Iain Campbell, the Regiment of Rannoch and Donald's Campbell's eyes have little control over tomorrow, for we fight forty thousand and we are three hundred souls. We must put our faith in the men from Scandinavia, the Welsh and their friends, the Irish boys and our own Highlanders and they know what they face tomorrow and we must have faith in the little stones that Tuppence and his guard stole from the dead and faith in Brendan's daughters for their magic might gain us surprise and Brendan's strategy might gain us superiority but if our imagination fails us, we are lost forever."

"I understand all you say, Luath, but my faith rests with you."

"You place a heavy burden, Iain Campbell."

"But I place it on you, do I not Am Mhathan?"

"You place it on me and I must accept but if we meet in Valhalla tomorrow evening do not be surprised."

AN CLAÒACh ÒEARG

The day dawned and the mist hung densely in the air. You could not see one hundred yards and I thought 'It will shield our movements till we form for battle and the sun will not burn the mist off the heather till we are set and ready'.

I was myself again for one mighty day of days. My preparations were simple and I prayed to none and I dressed for war.

I put on the colours that Uther's children wear because I am a child of Uther. Black, green and gold and the saffron robes of a Grandee. I wore no helm, like the Prince and no armour, and I drew the sword from the scabbard whose twin Iain Campbell now carried for Vulcan forged them together on the same morning in the same fire. I was ready now for battle.

Rannoch and Donald's Eyes had formed for the march to the shore land and I approached them slowly with Laggan by my side. They were silent and I stopped twenty yards in front and they said nothing but their eyes met mine and asked a thousand questions. We stood and looked at each other for a time, and then I spoke:

"You rogues from Rannoch, you brothers MacDonald, you Campbells with the Eyes for this Army, you Campbells of the Boar of

Cruachan, you daughters of Brendan the Pirate, precious jewels of Alexandria, you lads from Ulva with music in your hearts and in your fingers, Angus MacArthur my son the Bannerman, and Tuppence Why Montanus, Sarge and the King's Guard, I greet you all this misty morning."

"Your friend Luath regrets that he will not be with you this day. He has sent me to you in his stead. I pray you will not be disappointed."

Some call me Am Mhathan, The Bear, some call me Devil, some call me King, some call me Slayer of Saxons, but I, I am the son of Uther Pendragon, and I am the War Lord of the Celts and my father, he called me Arthur. I slept at Tri-Montium awaiting your call and I see they have returned to rape this land again. Well my friends let us welcome them to this Hell with fire and whistling steel."

Then the close company moved slowly towards me and Iain Campbell smiled and Aphra came to me and her long elegant black fingers touched the scars on my face and I bowed my head and she kissed my forehead and said:

"Your name we know now and it crosses oceans and continents and seas and echoes through the corridors of Time and floats in the dreams of Eternity. In the East my sisters and I have heard your name whispered softly, lest you hear; for what men see in you, men fear. We see the same as they, but what they fear, we love, for your honesty shines like a beacon across the gloomy skies of winter's night."

At that a runner came to us at speed shouting:

"Luath! Where is Luath?"

"He is not with us today, he rests."

"He cannot bloody rest, we have a battle to fight."

"He rests, I tell you."

"Aedan Bhan demands his presence on the field of battle immediately with his regiment. Our Army is formed up – we need him there now."

"He rests, I command this regiment today, and no living creature demands of Luath."

"And who are you?" I've never seen you before."

"Who I am matters little."

"What is your name runner?"

"My name is MacNeill, Dugald MacNeill."

"Well Dugald, you will be an Islesman from Barra no doubt?"

"Indeed, yes, I was born within sight of Kismuil's castle."

"Tell me this then MacNeill, where has Aedan Bhan placed the Campbells and the MacDonalds in the line this day?"

"As far away from each other as possible."

"Dugald, that's no use at all, return to Aedan Bhan and tell him to place the Campbells and the MacDonalds side by side today."

"Are you sure that's a good idea?"

"Positive, and tell Aedan to leave space for three hundred bang in the centre of the Highland line and this regiment will fill it shortly. And Dugald, you have a powerful voice?"

"Yes."

"In that case tell the Army that the War Lord is here, Arthur son of Uther Pendragon, I lead the Regiment of Rannoch this day."

"Am Mhathan?"

"Yes, Dugald, Am Mhathan!"

And Dugald MacNeill grasped my hands in his and looked me in the eyes and said:

"The Gods indeed smile upon us this day, our numbers have doubled this minute."

And Dugald left us at the run and Iain Campbell laughed, and said:

"Man or hound, there is no difference between the two of you. Luath does not rest. He is here today."

Tuppence spoke then with Sarge Montanus and the Guard in close attendance.

"Luath, sorry, Am Mhathan or is it Arthur, you've got an awful lot of different names. What do we call you?"

"Yes, what bleedin' name do we use?" said Sarge.

"Just pick one." I replied. "The choice is yours my little warriors."

Then, Tuppence, Sarge and the Guard had a little discussion amongst themselves.

"Can we just call you what your father called you?"

"Certainly."

"Good, that's a lot easier for us, we're happy now."

Dan and Eoin came closer with a question.

"Arthur?"

"Yes. Dan what is it?"

"There is some confusion here. Would you clarify the situation for the Campbell element of this army? You told Dugald MacNeill to tell Aedan Bhan to place the Campbells and the MacDonalds side by side in the line today?"

"Yes, I did."

"Is that not a recipe for disaster?" said Eoin.

"But you fought alongside MacDonalds today in this regiment, did you not?"

"Yes, but that's different we're friends."

"Put it this way, Dan. Is there pride in you for this name Campbell?"

"Most certainly!"

"And Ruiridh Mor are you proud of your name MacDonald?"

"Without question!"

"Well tell me this then. If the Campbells survive this day do you know one of them who will tell his grandchildren that the MacDonalds engaged the enemy first today, and do you think any MacDonald will tell his sons and his daughters that the Campbells outstripped them to the foe?"

"Point taken."

"Iain Campbell, you smile a lot these days?"

"I'm just enjoying myself Am Mhathan, that's all, and I'm learning the lessons from the master."

"Iain, these two great clans will never be united, but side by side they will strive to their utmost to be better than the other and they will sweep this army forward like a raging torrent and I for one would not care to be facing them."

Then we heard great cheering in the distance that just grew louder and louder.

"Dugald indeed communicates well. RANNOCH FORM UP! For that is our signal, let us proceed."

And we left Inistrynich and marched southwest with the finest pipers any regiment ever possessed and they played 'The Bonawe

Highlanders' and we passed Cladich where the Vikings were formed in a square on the left flank beside the river and three thousand cheered as we passed. Then we saw the Highland Line five thousand five deep and they stretched for one thousand yards from Cladich to Ardbrecknish and in the distance behind the mist were the Irish in a square on the right flank with four thousand and concealed behind Creag an Taghain to the rear of the Highland line were the Welsh and their friends from Cornwall, Brittany and the Basque country and we had our space, a gap for three hundred in the centre of the line and we filled it with Rannoch and on our right was Clan Donald and on our left was Clan Campbell and they cheered as we formed up and they threw each other looks that kill. We were here now at last and I stood beside Aedan Bhan in front of the Army and I remembered other armies and other friends and other battles.

Then slowly the mist began to clear and the day was beautiful as a day in May should be. But what we saw when the mist cleared took the breath away, for in front of us on Craig nan Sassanach formed in four mighty squares within a square was an army from a different place of forty thousand and they looked invincible and they had many banners and trumpets and they also had the high ground and I could feel our army's fears and frustration, but always it will be this way for little nations who dare to resist the Invader.

And Aedan turned to me and said:

"Are we lost Arthur or do we have a chance?"

"Aedan Bhan, Ard Righ na Alba we have no chance in Hell of defeating this Army unless we use the ultimate weapon."

"And what is that, Arthur?"

"Imagination."

And I turned to Rannoch and said:

"Are you complete and ready my friends?"

They roared back in the affirmative.

"In that case Angus unfurl The Blue Banner."

"Cara, did you give the Welsh their gifts from your father Brendan?"

"I did."

"And are they pleased, my girl?"

"They are as children with new toys."

"Good. Lu-an did every man in this Army drink from Bheithir's lost spring?"

"They did."

"And they all know the story?"

"They do."

"Good. Aphra did the Druids receive their gifts from your father?"

"Yes, Arthur they did."

"And do they understand the ritual?"

"They understand."

"Good, now we are ready."

And as I spoke the Army of the White Dragon began to move forward towards us and they move as always, slowly, one step at a time and they will not charge for I know them, they rely on overwhelming numbers and a compact and cohesive formation to grind enemies into defeat. Their shields were up and their spears were pointing forward and they will be with us shortly.

"Aedan, I think the time is upon us now."

Aedan Bhan then raised his hand in signal to the Druid of Carnac and upon that signal thirteen lesser Druids stepped out of the ranks along the whole front line of our Army and they all carried little caskets and they all took thirteen paces from the front rank then turned to face us. The Druid of Carnac went from casket to casket with The Stones of Tir-nan-Og on Danu's silver thread and placed one in each and poured Uisge Beatha over each stone till every casket contained a stone. He placed the blue stone in the casket in the centre of the army and the four amber in front of every thousand men in the Highland line. Two white he placed in front of the Vikings, the three green were for the Irish and one red in front of the Welsh. The black pearl he placed on the extreme left flank with the men from Scandinavia and the white pearl he placed on the extreme right flank with the men from Erinn. Then he spoke in a booming voice to a silent army with the enemy bearing down on them not three hundred yards away.

"Thirteen stones from Tir-nan-Og,
Stolen, at behest of Gods,
Carried here by birds of song,
To make this Army thrice as strong.
The battle plan we have is set,
But we have not the strength as yet,
But it will come and we will be,
The strongest foe they'll ever see.
See my priests consumed by fire,
With coloured stones of our desire.
Then children dear, your powers will grow
With every strike and every blow.
Led by heroes from the past,
White dragon there shall feel the blast.
And he will die upon this shore,
His fiery breath will burn no more."

Then thirteen other Druids stepped from the ranks carrying wands of fire and torched the caskets, and then retreated. Our army held its breath and waited for signs of fire. Their wait was short. The caskets fizzed and sparked, still held by the Druids as the fire consumed them.

The white smoke billowed upwards and a south-easterly breeze carried it to our foe and confusion reigned, then the smoke cleared and they saw what we saw.

In front of Rannoch stood in all his glory, the mighty Colkitto, Alasdair MacColla, Alasdair MacDonald the Younger of Colonsay and beside him on right and left were Red Hector MacLean of the Battles and the Mighty Somerled, Sorley, Lord of the Isles and the Bloody Major, Gilles Mor MacBean and the gruesome and terrible "Mad" Colin Campbell.

Five thousand roared their approval. These men were instantly recognised and five thousand broadswords beat on targes and the noise was deafening. Then the Irish joined in for they had in front of them Brian Boru and Conn of the Hundred Battles and Red Hugh O'Donnell. Then the Vikings joined the uproar as they had with them

Eric Blood Axe and Thorfinn the Mighty. Then the Welsh started singing for they had in front of them the legendary Owen Glendower. Then the noise increased again as the black pearl's persona was seen for it was Thorfinn Skullsplitter, axe in hand on a black chariot with a dragon head prow pulled by four black stallions prancing and neighing, desperate to be off. But the noise level hit a crescendo when the white pearl's persona appeared for it was none other than Sentanta, Cu Chulainn, the Hound of Coulann, the Beast of Ulster, the mightiest warrior of all, in a golden chariot clasping that infamous barbed spear Gay Bolga behind four milk white steeds of power and passion.

The first six ranks of the enemy had witnessed the whole affair and came to a juddering halt causing some confusion in the ranks to the rear and they partly lost their cohesion and discipline in the crush, and more importantly they were within in range of the Welsh bowmen.

"Now is the time Aedan Bhan, your army is strong and your enemy confused."

"Arthur, thank you, your word is ever true. Would you do me the honour of conducting this battle, for you are the War Lord?"

"It would be a pleasure."

"Tuppence, bring your guard in!"

"Yes, Sir."

And they flew in like lightning.

"We have formed our line, now we form our circle."

"Sarge Montanus, a serious commission for you."

"I've been waiting for this all bleedin' morning."

"Send one of your cohorts to each of our new recruits and tell them to proceed. Tell Owen Glendower to let his archers loose with their new toys and tell the Charioteers, Thorfinn and The Hound to fly and take their flankers round the enemies flanks and meet at the rear and when they meet you must inform them all for then and only then do we charge. And Sarge?"

"Yes, Arthur."

"Do not fail."

"Not bleedin' likely, Sir."

"Then go, for you start this battle my little friend and we will finish it."

In the twinkling of an eye the race was on, the Skullsplitter and Cu Chulainn flew round the flanks of the White Dragon and pulled the Norsemen and the Irish with them in a glorious manoeuvre that stretched our line into a circle. Our enemy reacted slowly and desperately tried to reform their ranks to face the encircling foe.

Glendower gave his orders and one thousand arrows fizzed and sparked as they flew over the heads of the Highlanders. They reacted with an almighty roar for they knew that fire would precede them as they charged. And these arrows struck home with a devastating effect in the heart of the enemy ranks. And men screamed and died in great numbers as Brendan's gifts were received. One thousand more from Owen within a minute and standards burnt and cloaks and clothing fired. A further thousand and the White Dragon lost shape and cohesion.

And then it happened, my greatest fear. Tuppence had joined his guard airborne without my knowledge and he was struck by a stray Welsh arrow and tumbled from the sky into the heart of enemy ranks and my stomach churned and my heart missed a beat and I must be strong.

And Rannoch reacted and moved forward and I roared at them.

"Stand fast, you bastards from the Moor and the Close Company hold on to your bloody discipline."

For if Rannoch went the whole line would go and it was too soon, only by minutes but too soon. Then I saw Sarge sweep down into the heart of the enemy and he came up alone and found my ear.

"There's no bleedin' sign of him Arthur, he's bleedin' lost and it's my fault."

"Montanus, you little bastard, you have a job to do. Do it!"

And Sarge Montanus looked into my eyes and said. "Yes, yes Sir, you are The Complete Bleedin' Bastard."

Then Aedan Bhan grabbed my arm and said to me:

"Arthur, I had a dream last night and I saw my two sons and one was dark haired and seventeen and the other was fourteen and I did not see his face but he is here today and his hands are the hands of a healer. And Arthur you know I have no wife and no sons and if I do not get through this day make Donald the King for he has knowledge beyond his years and the other boy, find him."

Burdens were placed upon me but at this moment Rannoch despised me and Tuppence was lost.

But Sarge Montanus came back to me and said:

"Arthur, the circle is complete."

"Well then my little friend, tell Alasdair MacColla, he stands in front of you now."

"Calum MacLean, your tune today, what is it?"

"'The Desperate Battle!'"

"Carry on MacLean."

And Sarge Montanus flew to Colkitto's ear and said:

"We have a circle, Alasdair."

"About bloody time, Montanus."

MacColla raised his hands, a broadsword in each and roared:

"CLAYMORE! CLAYMORE! CLAYMORE!"

And we charged, the complete circle together and the impact shook the ground beneath and Rannoch hit them first and went through the first five ranks like a reaper and Clan Donald and Clan Campbell had a devastating effect on the enemy as they struck together. Highland blades whistled and sang a beautiful tune this day, and Brendan's girls coloured the ground crimson with élan.

The Vikings hammered the enemy's right and rear till it buckled and distorted out of all recognition and as it caved in the screaming of the foe pierced the ears of Angels.

While the Irish just created bloody mayhem in their customary manner and green was not their colour today as they cut the enemy into ribbons of red and the men of Erinn had found their party and revelled in the slaughter of the Blackhearts.

There was no escape and a river of blood flowed slowly towards Bhiethir's Lost Spring.

Glendower's Welsh abandoned their longbows and took up the sword and came in behind Rannoch and together drove deep into the very heart of The Dragon. One enemy banner alone remained upright and they capitulated and discarded their weapons and fell on their knees and begged for mercy and they were given mercy, the seven thousand that remained alive. The slaughter ceased when Aedan Bhan raised his arms aloft and the battlefield fell silent and the silence was loud indeed, the silence broken only by the voice of Aedan and he said:

"Get off your knees Men of the White Dragon for you will be my messengers, you will leave this land and return home and tell your peoples what happened here at the Red Shore and do not let them ever forget."

Then Aedan saw a young boy standing beside the remaining standard that still flew and the boy had his hands clasped close to his chest.

"What is so precious that you carry it next to your heart?"

"Life," said the boy.

And he opened his hands and said, "I did not want the little bird to die."

And Tuppence flew up out of the boy's hands without a mark on him.

"Luath are you alright?"

"I'm fine my little friend but how are you?"

"Grand, couldn't be better, but where have all the Heroes gone, Luath?"

"I see none but Heroes on this bloody field, Tuppence. Come my friend, let us go home."

And we turned and left An Cladach Dearg and as we moved away Aedan Bhan called out:

"Tuppence Why Montanus High King of The Sparrows you forgot something."

We turned round and Aedan Bhan was standing with his right arm in the air and his bloodied fist clenched and Tuppence flew back to him and slowly he uncurled his fingers and in the palm of his hand was a silver thread with thirteen little stones on it – one blue, four amber, three green, two white, one red and one black pearl and one white pearl.

The End